ROBERT GOLUBA

Absolute Command

A Christian Suspense Novella

First published by Evertouch Publishing, an imprint of Evertouch Inc 2020

Copyright © 2020 by Robert Goluba

All rights reserved. No part of this publication may be reproduced, stored or transmitted in any form or by any means, electronic, mechanical, photocopying, recording, scanning, or otherwise without written permission from the publisher. It is illegal to copy this book, post it to a website, or distribute it by any other means without permission.

This novel is entirely a work of fiction. The names, characters and incidents portrayed in it are the work of the author's imagination. Any resemblance to actual persons, living or dead, events or localities is entirely coincidental.

First edition

ISBN: 978-1-7330513-3-0

This book was professionally typeset on Reedsy. Find out more at reedsy.com

Contents

Acknowledgement	v
Connect with Me	vi
Chapter 1	1
Chapter 2	5
Chapter 3	10
Chapter 4	15
Chapter 5	20
Chapter 6	25
Chapter 7	28
Chapter 8	33
Chapter 9	37
Chapter 10	42
Chapter 11	47
Chapter 12	55
Chapter 13	58
Chapter 14	63
Chapter 15	68
Chapter 16	72
Chapter 17	76
Chapter 18	80
Chapter 19	84
Chapter 20	86
Chapter 21	91
Chapter 22	96
Chapter 23	102
Chapter 24	107

Chapter 25	111
Chapter 26	118
Dangerous Redemption Collection	122
Connect With Me	124
About the Author	125
Also by Robert Goluba	126

Acknowledgement

Thank you to everyone that helped create Absolute Command and launch the Dangerous Redemption Collection.
Edited by Laurel Garver

Cover Design by Stephen Novak

Connect with Me

Join My New Release Text List

Text **NEW** to **(844) 465-7100** to receive a text notification of each of my new releases. Nothing else. Ever.

Sign up for the new release and promotion notification newsletter at: **RobertGoluba.com/newletter**

Chapter 1

John Nickerson closed his eyes and inhaled the sweet aroma of fresh-cut grass before he curled his gloved hand around the brass handle of the casket. His eyelids shot open when he felt the casket rise from the stand under the strength of the other pallbearers. Together they slid the seven-foot-long chest draped in a United States flag into the rear cavern of a black hearse.

After the back door swung closed, John took a last look at the red, white, and blue through the tinted glass. He wobbled across the crumbling asphalt in the parking lot until his wife Stacy intercepted him. Wispy strands of auburn hair that had escaped her tight bun bounced with every step. Yards from their vehicle, she caught John and locked her right arm with his left and continued with him to their SUV.

A blast of heat, the handiwork of the Texas sun in early May, pushed John like an invisible hand when he opened the door. John turned the ignition and cranked the air conditioner to maximum output. His curly golden hair danced in the artificial gust.

"Are you okay?" Stacy asked.

"No. I'm not."

"We can just sit here until you're ready."

John stared ahead. Beyond the windshield, the rest of the mourners were entering their cars, but he didn't really see them. He only saw the closed eyes of twenty-three-year-old Kyle Rhodes in his Army dress uniform, laying in permanent sleep on a silky white pillow.

John's nephew. The son of his big sister Kayla and his brother-in-law Frank. Kyle survived two tours with the US Army in the Middle East, but not the impact of a box truck while driving through an intersection in Austin, Texas.

"I'm so sorry, Kyle. May you be wrapped in the arms of Jesus as you enter His Kingdom," John whispered.

"Sorry? What did you say?" Stacy inquired.

"I'm ready to go now."

The Nickersons joined the procession to the cemetery. John's mind was still on Kyle as he maintained a subconscious car length from the bumper in front of him.

Images of Kyle flashed in John's mind. He remembered watching Kyle on Christmas morning and the excitement he had when he discovered his bounty of toys. John always looked forward to the annual fishing trips with Frank and Kyle before he had children of his own. It was a special time for him, and Kyle was always a big reason why.

After John got married and started to have kids of his own, he didn't spend as much time with Kyle. John always maintained a strong relationship with his older sister and considered Frank to be a close friend, especially after John and Stacy moved into their neighborhood. As a neighbor and uncle, John watched Kyle turn into a young man during his teenage years. He was good-looking, active with his church, and well-liked by the kids his age. John smiled whenever he saw Kyle drive past his house in his fixed-up Chevy truck with country music blaring for

CHAPTER 1

the whole neighborhood to enjoy. After he returned from his service with the Army in the Middle East, Kyle was attending community college to pursue his degree in law enforcement.

Kyle had a bright future, but he died a very preventable death.

The driver of the box truck responsible for the collision never should have been behind the wheel of the unsuspecting murder weapon. The driver was preparing to stand trial at the Municipal Courthouse in downtown Austin for felony drug possession when he slipped away from the judicial department staff unnoticed. He wiggled out of his decade's old shackles and chains. It could have been a simple walk-away escape, but he carjacked a box truck from a uniform delivery service parked near the courthouse.

The compounding crimes caught the attention of the judicial staff, and they notified the Austin police. A pursuit ensued.

The inmate who should have been secured in his handcuffs as he waited to be sentenced was racing down crowded streets in Austin in his orange prison suit.

Luck was on the side of many other Austin citizens that morning as the inmate in the box truck blew through multiple red lights in his attempt to flee the police. Kyle Rhodes was not so lucky. Four minutes after the inmate stole the box truck, it entered the same intersection that Kyle was crossing. The collision immediately extinguished the bright light of Kyle Rhodes on his way to work.

The red glow of brake lights jerked John back to his journey to the cemetery.

"I need to do something about this," John blurted.

"What can you do?" Stacy asked.

"I'm not sure yet. They said on the news that the inmate slipped out of his shackles because they have been using the same sets of restraints for over a decade. There has to be a better way to secure an inmate than to use first-century technology."

Stacy put her hand on his. "You always have excellent ideas. I'm sure you'll think of something."

"I work for a security company. You'd think someone at Fletcher Security would come up with a better solution than metal hand and leg cuffs."

Stacy squeezed John's hand and nodded as they slowed to enter the cemetery. Neither spoke again until they parked and joined the rest of the mourners.

John was present when they laid Kyle to rest, but only physically. He was deep in his head, mentally a million miles away. John was in a place that ran through potential solutions that would prevent a tragedy like Kyle's from happening again.

One idea stood out among all others.

Chapter 2

John arrived at his desk at Fletcher Security two days later. The sobs of his sister Kayla and the dried trail of tears on Frank's cheek were still fresh in his mind. The loss of their only child was a pain that John couldn't comprehend, nor did he want to.

John picked up a picture on his desk of his three children. The mischievous smiles of his two sons and one daughter on the beach as they squinted looking into the sun made his heart throb for his sister's family. Nobody should have to endure that agony.

He put the picture back down and recalled the lengthy list of new product ideas he'd dreamed up.

The desire to create better security solutions was not new to John. He has shared dozens of his ideas with the president and founder of the company, Karl Fletcher, and not once had the boss expressed interest.

After each suggestion from John, the company owner replied the same way: "You're a software engineer. You focus on that and let us come up with the new products, and we'll let you help us bring them to life."

The condescending tone of Karl Fletcher's response penetrated John's bones like the harsh scraping of a metal fork across a dinner plate. The lack of consideration made it harder for

John to recommend anything beneficial to Mr. Fletcher.

Despite his weariness with Karl Fletcher's aloof reactions, John wasn't deterred. The thought of visiting Kayla and Frank's house with Kyle gone forever caused his chest to ache. If he could prevent another family from experiencing the deep sense of loss as his sister and brother-in-law, it was worth all his efforts.

John examined new algorithms on his computer. How could he have prevented this tragedy?

"Hey, buddy, glad to have you back. We were swamped without you."

The familiar voice was a welcome sound for John. It was Raj, a fellow programmer at Fletcher Security.

"Hey, Raj. The last two days have been hard. Thanks for covering for me."

"No problem. I'm glad I could help," Raj replied with a hint of his Indian accent still evident despite living in Texas over twenty years.

"The time away got me thinking again."

"Uh-oh, what new product are you going to show Mr. Fletcher this time?"

"I'm serious. I need to create a better solution to detain inmates, so no family has to go through this again."

The smile once prominent on Raj's face faded as his expression turned serious. "That's great. Don't give up on your new products because Mr. Fletcher doesn't see the value in any of them."

"I'm not talking about new products."

Raj's brows pinched, and his forehead wrinkled. "What then are you talking about?

"I'm talking about starting my own business, so I can launch my own product ideas. I'm not doing the world any favors by keeping all my ideas in my head."

"You should do it. You could build an impressive company," Raj replied with the genuine sincerity of a brother.

John wished he shared the same confidence in himself. He'd wanted to build his own company since he graduated from the University of Texas fifteen years ago. *Not ready, not enough money, and not a good enough idea* were regular thoughts that thwarted his business ventures. Now thirty-seven and a husband and father of three children, he knew starting a new business today would be a monumental challenge.

John planned to share his ideas with Stacy. He hoped that if she supported his new concept, it would give him the confidence he needed to pursue his own business.

After they put their three children to bed, John joined Stacy on the family room couch. She was watching the evening news while she scrolled through her phone.

"Hey, Hon, you got a second?"

"Sure," Stacy replied. She set her phone on the coffee table and turned toward John.

"You know how I've always told you about my ideas for new products," he began, "and you've mentioned that I may want to sell those ideas to someone else?"

Stacy nodded.

"I've been thinking that now may be the time to sell my ideas and start a business of my own. What do you think about launching a company to pursue some of my new product ideas?"

Stacy pursed her lips and crossed her arms. She stared at the pictures of their three smiling children on the wall next to the TV. A moment later, she raised her chin and then lowered it as if she had the answer to the question she'd asked her inner self.

"I've always thought you would be a great business owner, and I think some of your product ideas could be big hits, but starting a business is a big commitment. I have a lot of questions."

John nodded. "I know it is. What questions do you have?"

"You're not planning to just quit your job, are you?

"Oh, no. I want to keep working as long as I can. I can start a new business on the side."

Stacy crossed her legs. "What about all the money you'll need to start a new business and get it off the ground? Where is that money going to come from?"

"I'm going to do some research on loans and I'll look for a few investors once I get started, but I was hoping we could use some of the money we set aside for a future business."

Stacy stared at John for what seemed like a full minute. She exhaled and responded, "I'm okay with you pursuing your own business as long as you understand the health and financial wellbeing of the kids is still your number one priority."

"Of course," John said as he moved closer to Stacy on the couch.

"We can use what we've saved up for one of your business projects, but it's not a lot. A new business can burn through that like a brush fire on a dry Texas day. My income working at Doctor Beasley's office helps, but I can't cover even half of our expenses on my salary. You need a plan to fund your business beyond our savings."

John leaned over and planted a kiss on Stacy's lips and followed up with a tight hug. He pulled back, "I understand all of your concerns. I'll be cautious with our savings, and I'll start to look for new funding. It will be nice to reap some of the financial rewards from my ideas."

The next day John began scratching out a business plan on

CHAPTER 2

the back of the electric bill. He'd been at this place before, many times, but this time was different. John didn't just want to start his own business. He had to. The prevention of another tragedy like Kyle's was at stake.

Chapter 3

A reminder popped up on John's screen when he logged in at work.

"Oh, no, I forgot about this."

John had to meet with Karl Fletcher, the director of sales, and the finance manager for an on-site sales call in an hour. The meeting was to review an RFP from the Travis County Correctional Complex with the opportunity to replace their existing security system. It was an enormous opportunity for the company, so Mr. Fletcher wanted to have a full team on location with him.

One hour later, the four Fletcher employees met in the lobby and followed the sales director to his truck. During the thirty-minute drive to the Travis County Correctional Complex or TCCC out past the Austin Airport, Karl Fletcher reminded everyone multiple times about the importance of the account.

"We need to sharpen our pencil on this one, so everyone here needs to understand each nuance of the RFP and what it will cost us," Mr. Fletcher reminded the team.

That was why John was part of the Fletcher Security entourage. As a software engineer, he had to estimate the cost of all the programming to replace the aging security system in the complex.

CHAPTER 3

The first hour of the meeting took place in a typical board room near the entrance of the complex. The Travis County purchasing department answered questions regarding the contents and expectations in the RFP that was as thick as a college textbook.

John helped himself to a second cup of coffee to remain alert as the meeting droned on. His eyelids felt heavier every minute the discussion touched on subjects like expense tracking spreadsheets, waterfall charts, and building diagrams.

After sixty minutes passed, everyone stood up. John was looking forward to going back to the office to analyze his notes, but their meeting was not over.

"Time for a tour of the facility."

John felt a warm sensation rush from his chest to his toes. He put down his coffee. He no longer needed it.

The safety manager for TCCC entered and asked everyone to take their seats. He barked out the rules for entering the secure portion of the complex. His cadence reminded John of one of his drill sergeants during Army basic training twenty years earlier.

"You may encounter an inmate during the tour. Do not talk to him or look him in the eye. Just stay out of the way and let our corrections officers do their jobs. If you follow all the rules I've shared, you'll all go home tonight in one piece to kiss your husband, wife, girlfriend, boyfriend, or dog good night. I haven't lost anyone yet, and I don't intend to today."

John's palms were sweating. The sales director and Mr. Fletcher simply smirked. They saw nothing inside those walls other than dollar signs. The finance manager Amber, on the other hand, looked pale as she tapped her foot during the safety briefing. Once the door buzzed open, John fell back to be next to Amber. Misery and fear loved company.

The party of five navigated the rectangular complex without incident. They stopped at every door and analyzed the existing security equipment. Over time, John relaxed, and he sensed Amber did the same.

They were two doors away from the exit when John heard someone behind them shout.

"On your left."

The safety manager ordered everyone to move to the right and against the wall. Two corrections officers had one inmate in an orange jumpsuit between them, headed toward the transport dock. The trio passed Mr. Fletcher and the sales director without breaking stride, but that changed once the inmate noticed Amber. She was in her early thirties, and her long chestnut-brown hair draped across her white blazer. The inmate tried to stop, but the corrections officers tightened their grip to keep his momentum heading in the right direction. The inmate must have decided he wanted to talk to Amber above all else, because he thrashed his arms and elbows until one of the corrections officers lost his grip.

Despite his handcuffed hands in front of him, the inmate inched closer to Amber. She made eye contact with him, and that was like tossing gas on a bonfire. He broke free from the other officer.

Untethered from the officers, the inmate fixed his gaze on Amber and shuffled toward her. John moved in front of Amber and extended his arm in a stop position like a police officer directing traffic. He didn't have a plan. He just knew that someone had to stop this man before he reached Amber. John tensed every muscle in his body and waited for impact.

As the inmate charged, John counted down the steps before

he felt the weight of the inmate on him. Four, three, two—.

The inmate's handcuffed arms stretched out like a zombie, and his fingers grasped John's shirt. Instead of hitting John head-on, the inmate reached for him as he altered his course.

The inmate's hair smacked John in the cheek as the safety director tackled him and brought him down to the concrete floor with a thud. Seconds later, the two correction officers jumped on him. Everyone was shouting, and then ten seconds later it turned quiet.

The safety manager held the inmate in a headlock and turned to a corrections officer.

"You got this now?"

"Yes, sir," one of them replied.

"Okay, hang tight with him until I get these civilians out of here."

The ride back to the Fletcher Security office was quiet. The hum of the off-road tires on the concrete highway was the only sound in the cab.

John assumed Karl Fletcher and the sales director were running profit projections in their heads. He looked over at Amber and saw her staring out the window like an innocent child. It made John's heart sink. He felt sorry that she had been targeted behind the walls of TCCC, now growing smaller in the rear-view mirror.

Outrage pushed aside sympathy for Amber. The officers at TCCC might have prevented the incident if they had the right equipment and tools to handle the transport of inmates. Why were they still using ancient technology and expecting different results?

John looked out his window at the passing buildings. First, it was Kyle and now Amber. When was someone going to provide a solution that worked?

John made a fist in each hand. Resolve pumped through his veins like electricity.

The answer John was seeking was clear.

Nobody else was going to provide the solution. It had to be him.

Chapter 4

The new transmitters from the Fletcher Security supply closet sat on John's desk. He arranged them in random shapes while he thought of the possibilities. He had to create a product that could accomplish two unique objectives. One aim was to find a better way to secure individuals in the custody of law enforcement. The other was a flagship product worthy of launching a new company.

Every security firm in the area offered the standard RFID scan cards for secure building access and now most offered the latest biometric scanners. John had to go one step further. He needed a product line that would catapult his company right out of the gate.

John whispered to himself as he tilted his head and squinted at the rice-sized transmitters. "Instead of keeping people out, I can focus on keeping people in. I'm sure my sister would agree our industry can do a better job there."

He leaned back in his chair and interlocked his fingers behind his head. The suppliers of the transmitters on his desk said they were the first of their kind in America. A German company manufactured them, and their research teams had tested a variety of novel uses that John had never seen before. A test that caught John's eye was one in which the transmitter could automatically close and lock a door. John sprang forward and picked up a transmitter.

Could they do the same thing to a human? Can they pull wrists or arms next to a torso?

A flood of ideas poured into John's mind. This could be the breakthrough product he needed. John opened his browser and found the manufacturer's website. For the next ninety minutes, he studied the technical specs of this futuristic technology.

John was so engrossed with his new findings that he didn't hear Karl Fletcher come into the engineering office. He was standing behind John before he was able to push the transmitters to the side.

Mr. Fletcher pointed to the transmitters on John's desk. "What's that?"

"Those are the transmitters we received from that new German supplier. I've been doing some research on them, and they can do several things that our current products can't do."

"Like what?"

"They can help close doors and keep them secure so nobody can gain access to a classified area because of an accidental open door. I believe they could lead to an entire line of products to secure things inside facilities."

"That's a pipedream," Mr. Fletcher scoffed. "Fletcher Security has flourished by focusing on keeping people out of buildings, rooms, and areas where they don't belong. Nobody cares about closing open doors."

His boss's harsh tone, and obliviousness to how his dismissal contradicted itself made John's heart sink. Disappointment pulsed throughout his body. What use was it to argue? He simply mumbled, "Yes, sir."

When John looked up, Mr. Fletcher was standing behind

another software engineer critiquing the work on his screen.

He wasn't surprised Mr. Fletcher shot down his idea for a new product because that always happened, but this rejection stung more than usual. John believed that the transmitters were a unique solution that could help thousands of companies and people.

John pushed the transmitters aside and focused on his growing list of software projects nearing their deadline. Three hours later, John submitted his last project for the day. Most of his co-workers had left for home. He turned his attention back to the transmitters.

"Fletcher may not like my idea, but I know it can solve a problem."

The office was tranquil except for the pecking of the keyboard coming from John's desk. He was sending code to the main transmitter. Before he clicked his mouse to conduct his test, John got up and walked around the office. He didn't find another soul at their desk, so he wandered up to the reception area to get a better view of the parking lot. His white Ford SUV cast a long solitary shadow across the asphalt lot. A blinking light that signaled that the office's front door was armed was the only other activity in the building. John scurried back to his desk. He hovered the mouse over the send button and clicked it.

Two transmitters raced across his desk and crashed into each other.

John jumped from his chair with his fists in the air.

"It works!"

John sat down as if his yell would bring him unwanted attention, but the whir of the fan in his laptop was the only other sound in the room. He pushed the transmitters into his desk drawer and powered down his computer.

"I've got to tell Stacy. This could be the ticket to my own business."

John crept through the door when he got home. He saw evidence of an attempted family dinner on the kitchen table and stovetop. The sounds of boys laughing came from the back hallway. When John opened a bedroom door, he found his oldest son Connor trying to ride his younger brother Zach like a rodeo bull.

"Come on, Zach, you can do better than that," the eleven-year-old bellowed to his brother two years his junior.

"Connor, get off your brother. Where's Mom?"

Connor slid off Zach's back and plopped to the floor. "She's giving Abby a bath."

John walked down the hall and opened the door with a smile. He'd been excited to share his findings with Stacy the entire drive home.

"Do you have a minute?"

Stacy rinsed Abby's hair and twisted her brown locks to wring out the excess bathwater.

"I don't," Stacy growled. "It's past Abby's bedtime, and I still need to get her dried off and in her PJs. The boys have been ignoring me all night, so they're your problem now. They need to get their showers and get ready for bed."

John opened his mouth but closed it without uttering a word. Stacy worked part-time as an office manager at a local dental office. She was taking care of the house and kids with limited help from her husband on most nights. John realized he had to chip in and help his soul mate.

"Got it. Sorry I got home so late. I was brainstorming and lost track of time."

CHAPTER 4

Stacy toweled off Abby, refusing to acknowledge his excuse.

After the once rowdy house turned quiet, John joined Stacy in the bedroom. She was already in bed reading a book. He completed his nightly bedtime routine and slid under the covers next to Stacy.

She put her book down. "Did you have something to tell me tonight?"

"It wasn't anything important."

"Are you sure? You seemed like you needed to tell me something when you came home."

He shrugged. "Yeah, I'm just kicking something around. Nothing more than that."

John stared into the blackness. It was true; he didn't have relevant news to share with Stacy, just another idea that excited him. He needed to be extra sure about his idea this time.

Chapter 5

The entire office at Fletcher Security crowded into the loading dock just before ten. They waited for their leader to emerge for their all-company meeting. Karl Fletcher bounced from the side door with a wide smile.

"Good morning, ladies and gentlemen. I have monumental news. We completed the financial reports from the prior fiscal year, and the results exceeded our projections by over twenty percent."

The slender man with short, curly strawberry blonde hair paced like a tiger in a zoo in front of three work vans bearing logos with his family name. He shared a half dozen key events that led to revenue beating expectations.

"That's not the only good news."

Mr. Fletcher paused to create additional suspense.

"The entire Fletcher Security team will benefit from these results. Everyone will receive their standard bonus plus an extra twenty percent this year for the exceptional results."

The loading dock erupted with cheers. Some co-workers exchanged high fives while other shared hugs. The news conflicted John. He was ecstatic about the extra money, but leaving Fletcher Security to start his own business just got tougher. It would be harder to convince Stacy that now was a good time to walk away from the financial security of his current job.

John returned to his desk and spent the rest of the morning updating reports on the status of his projects. After lunch, he began writing code for an urgent project but stopped after thirty minutes. He opened his desk drawer. The sight of the transmitters curved his lips upward.

Raj and the other programmers were still out to lunch, so he pulled out the transmitters again. This time he created a program for six transmitters to unite on command. Once his code was complete, John looked around the room to verify it was clear. He clicked his mouse, and the six transmitters snapped together to form three clusters. John stood and took a lap around the office. He would tell Stacy about his exciting discovery tonight.

John left work at precisely five o'clock so he'd be home in time to help Stacy with dinner and the kids. He didn't want a repeat of the night before.

Once he shut all three bedroom doors, John joined Stacy on the family room couch. He pretended to watch the evening news with her, but he couldn't contain his true intentions any longer.

"I have some good news and some great news to share with you."

Stacy smiled and hopped over one cushion to be closer to John.

"Okay, what is it?"

"Fletcher Security beat the sales projections by so much this year that we will get an extra twenty percent in our annual bonuses."

Stacy slung her arms around John and kissed him. "That is

marvelous news. We could use that extra cash right now."

"I know. It was unexpected, which made it even sweeter."

"I bet."

"I have more great news."

"Better than that? Tell me now."

"I think I've found my flagship product to help me launch my own business."

Stacy's smile disappeared. "What is it?"

John looked around and grabbed two magazines from the side of the couch and put them on the coffee table.

"I've found a supplier that has created transmitters that can pull them together with substantial force when activated. There is nothing else like it in the industry." John pushed the two magazines together to demonstrate.

Stacy moved back to her original location on the opposite end of the couch. "I don't understand. What's the benefit?"

"The benefit?" John's nose pinched as he furrowed his brow. "The benefit is that it can help secure or detain someone. If that guy who killed Kyle had something like this, he never would have escaped, and Kyle would still be here today."

Stacy stared at the spine of the cooking magazine butted up against the spine of the home décor magazine on her coffee table.

"Okay, I can see the benefit now, but is that enough to start a new business? You are making more than ever at Fletcher."

John couldn't find the words to respond. He pictured the conversation unfolding in a much different manner when he thought about it earlier that day. Now Stacy was questioning the viability of the product he was so excited about five minutes earlier. It was like telling Mr. Fletcher all over again.

John stood up and started toward the bedroom. "Maybe

you're right."

"Don't get mad. I just want to be sure you have thought everything through before you jump to something new."

"Okay, I'll conduct thorough diligence before I jump into anything."

John lay awake for hours after he pulled the comforter up to his chin. He ran a million scenarios through his head. The transmitters still felt like the right idea, so John prayed for guidance. "Lord, help me find the path you've paved for me."

The next morning before work, John was less talkative than usual. He scrolled through his phone in the kitchen without saying a word to Stacy.

Stacy put down her coffee. "Are you still mad?"

"I'm not mad. Just disappointed."

"I guess I just don't really understand what you've created."

John locked eyes with Stacy. Convinced she was sincere, he explained his idea again.

"The transmitters I tested will create a product that can vastly improve how we secure people like inmates and detainees. A handful of these new transmitters would create a virtual straitjacket on a person when activated. Therefore, we wouldn't have any more police pursuits of someone who slipped out of traditional shackles or got away during transport. The inmate would be completely subdued by these new transmitters."

Stacy nodded first and then smiled.

"That makes a lot more sense now. I just didn't understand your idea last night."

John exhaled. "I know it's still very rough, and I have a lot more testing to do, but starting my own business is very important to me. I think this could be the breakthrough product I need to do it."

Stacy rose from her chair and walked over to her husband. She put her hands on each side of his waist and looked into his eyes.

"I know this is about more than starting a new business. I understand that you *have* to do this. You need to prove to yourself what the rest of us already know. You have amazing ideas for products that will make the world a better place, and you need to bring one of those products to life for you to believe it."

John didn't respond. Stacy exposed a secret that he thought was artfully tucked away and hidden from anyone. Her comment left him disturbed.

Chapter 6

John sat down at his desk with a renewed sense of conviction. The support of Stacy was the nudge he needed to understand the potential of his new idea. He didn't want to let her down.

Mid-morning, John opened his desk drawer to peek at the transmitters. He had to do more testing to ensure this concept was the right one to launch his business. John assembled six transmitters on the left side of his desk and then looked around the engineering office. Everyone was busy.

I really should test these at home.

The allure of an immediate answer to his question was more than John was able to resist. He positioned each transmitter to represent an area on the human body. The elbow, wrist, and knee on both the right and left side to simulate a virtual straitjacket once activated.

While John was assembling the transmitters in the proper locations, he felt a hand on his shoulder. John jumped and turned around to see his coworker Raj standing behind him.

"What are you doing?"

John saw that Raj was looking at his transmitters. He considered sweeping them into his desk drawer and telling Raj that it was nothing, but John yearned to receive feedback from somebody else.

"These are the new transmitters from that German supplier. I've been playing with some ideas on how to utilize these in a new product."

"What do you have so far?"

"Give me a second, and I'll show you."

John turned back to his keyboard and typed in a few new commands. He moved his mouse over the submit button and turned his chair to face Raj.

"Watch this."

John hit the submit button, and with a faint clicking sound, the six transmitters became three pairs of transmitters as they joined each other.

"Whoa!"

"Pretty cool, huh?"

"Yeah, but how will you use it?"

"I have a few ideas. One of them is like a virtual straitjacket."

John crossed his arms tight like a strong self-bear hug to show how it may look. "It would allow law enforcement to secure someone so they could no longer resist or flee."

"That's great. You may be onto something this time. It's about time you came up with a new idea around here," Raj said with a sheepish grin.

John leaned back in his chair to gloat. Just as he did, he noticed Karl Fletcher enter the engineering office. Raj quickly turned and snuck back to his desk. John leaned forward to swipe the transmitters off his desktop and into his drawer, but it was too late. Mr. Fletcher was on him like a cheetah on a gazelle.

"How's it going, fellas?" Mr. Fletcher asked. Before John could answer, Karl Fletcher noticed the transmitters on his desk.

CHAPTER 6

"I thought I told you we already have too many new products in the pipeline. We have more than we can even create now. Why are you wasting your time on something like this?"

John brushed the transmitters into his desk and closed it.

"I'm sorry. It won't happen again."

"It better not!"

Mr. Fletcher's forehead turned from a light beige to bright red. "We have a lot to do this year to achieve the same results as last year. We all need to give one hundred percent every minute of every day when we are in this office. I can't have an engineer on my team going rogue on me and working on projects that are not aligned with the company's objectives. Don't let me see those transmitters again."

Mr. Fletcher stomped out of the room. John knew a crossroads was in his near future. He wasn't sure if he was ready.

Chapter 7

John sat motionless for several minutes after Mr. Fletcher left the engineering office. He stared at the blue light radiating from the large monitor on his desk but saw nothing. The only other sound in the room was the tapping of keys, followed by an occasional mouse click.

The silence was broken by the sound of his desk drawer sliding open until it caught on the stop. John rummaged through the drawer until he found a small box with two remaining pens.

"Perfect."

He dumped the pens into the drawer and replaced them with the transmitters. John closed the top of the box and placed it in his backpack. Raj arrived next to John as he zipped it up.

"What are you going to do now?"

John shook his head. "I've been thinking about this for a while. I'll do everything at home. It's what I should've done in the first place—experiment on my own time in my own space."

After work, John rushed home to the fifth bedroom. He and Stacy had long discussed making it a guest bedroom, but because they didn't have a basement, it morphed into a disorganized storage mess.

John surveyed the scene after he opened the door. "Do we

CHAPTER 7

ever throw anything away?"

Once the dread of the scene washed over John, he got to work. He pulled a dozen boxes, storage containers, and countless old coats off the queen size bed. He stacked them high against the wall, and then he pushed the mattress and box spring up until they rested next to an adjacent wall. The forty square feet hidden under the bed was John's new workspace. After finding two legs from an old dining room table and a sheet of plywood decorated with puddles of dry paint in the garage, his first research lab was complete. Or almost complete.

John found Stacy in the kitchen.

"Doesn't Doctor Beasley's wife own a women's boutique?"

She leaned against the counter and wiped her hands on a towel. "Yeah, why?"

"Can you see if they'll give or sell me an old mannequin?

"A mannequin?"

"Yes, I need something with arms and hands so I can test my new transmitters."

"Okay, I'll ask."

Two days later, John arrived from work and turned on the light to his lab. He jumped back and grabbed his chest. A human head was lying on its side on his makeshift table with eyes wide open.

John exhaled after his eyes adjusted. It was the mannequin he requested. He yelled down the hall. "Thanks, Honey!"

Thirty minutes later, he had the former brunette model assembled and seated in a chair. The mannequin was too old and flimsy to stand without additional support, so John would have to test it sitting down. The shoulder joints were badly worn, which caused the arms to flop wildly every time John touched the mannequin. Perfect for his test.

John spent the next sixty minutes taping the transmitters on the wrists and elbows of his test subject. After he was satisfied, John lined up each transmitter in the correct location and opened his laptop on top of the plywood surface. The code to activate the transmitters filled his screen. His first test was minutes away.

John positioned his cursor above the activate button. He exhaled and rubbed his hands together. This was the moment of truth. Just before he could click his mouse, the door burst open. Connor was chasing Zach with a brown bag in his outstretched arms. Zach cried that he didn't want to eat worms.

John stood up. "What's wrong, Zach?"

"Connor is trying to make me eat worms."

"They're gummy worms," Connor said with a smile.

"I still don't want to eat them. They look gross."

Connor dangled a gummy worm between his thumb and index finger and started toward Zach again. His younger brother turned and ran toward their father for protection. Zach knocked the mannequin off the chair, and transmitters flew everywhere.

"Connor, drop those worms right now!" John roared.

Both boys froze in place. John pulled Zach from behind his workspace and placed the two boys together.

"I'm trying to work here, and I don't need you two fighting with each other in here or anywhere in this house. I don't want to see any more teasing or chasing."

Their heads dropped, and they both stared at the floor.

"Dad, we're bored," Connor said.

"You need to find a better way to entertain yourself. Now, you're both going to bed early tonight. Go get your PJs on, brush your teeth, and be in bed in twenty minutes."

CHAPTER 7

"But dad, my bedtime is not for another two hours," Connor protested.

"I don't care. When you horse around like you did here, you go to bed early. Come on, let's get going. You only have nineteen minutes left before I come back to make sure you are in bed."

The boys shuffled down the hall, and John assessed the damage. He picked the mannequin back up and looked out the window. A half dozen neighbor boys and girls were out playing in the waning minutes of daylight. John shook his head and let his chin drop to his chest. The boys were never going to sleep unless they ran off the excess energy that had them fighting in the first place. They needed better solutions to their problem, not harsher punishment.

John exhaled and walked down the hallway. Connor and Zach were standing in front of the sink with their toothbrushes.

"I need both of you to stop brushing your teeth."

"It hasn't been twenty minutes yet," Zach reminded his father.

"I know, but I need two boys to be brown bear cubs. I'm a zookeeper and I need to catch two runaways. You two get a thirty-second head start to go outside and hide because when I come looking for you, I will put you in back in the zoo when I catch you."

Zach and Connor looked at each other with furrowed brows.

"You better get going. Twenty-nine, twenty-eight—"

Broad smiles appeared on the faces of both boys as they darted toward the front door. They howled with joy as they burst out the door and into their yard.

Stacy came out from Abby's room into the hallway.

"I heard yelling. What's wrong?"

"Nothing's wrong. I'm going to play with the boys for a while before they go to bed."

"I thought you have a lot of work to do."

John leaned over and kissed Stacy's temple. He was ready to start his pursuit of the bear cubs.

"I do. In fact, I have a ton of work to do."

John opened the door, paused, and turned back to Stacy. "This is just more important."

Chapter 8

John finished putting the mannequin back together, and the transmitters in the right locations as the first rays of sun entered his lab. After playing with Connor and Zach the previous evening, John committed to pursuing this new product idea, but not at the expense of spending time with his family. He had a full-time job and was adding a second. More predawn mornings and late nights were in his future.

John finished the code, and this time he hit the submit button a second later to avoid any new last-minute catastrophes. The right arm and wrist slammed into the mannequin's torso as instructed, but the left arm did not move. John reread his code and clicked the submit button again. After the third time, John threw his hands in the air.

"Why isn't this working?"

Ten minutes and four more tries later, John heard a tap at his door.

"Come in."

Stacy stuck her head in the lab. "Are you going to work today?"

John looked down at his watch. "Shoot, I've got to get going." He slid his laptop into his backpack and headed to the kitchen to grab a banana.

"Thanks for the reminder, hon. I'll be home for dinner."

At the office, John immersed himself into his overflowing list of projects. His growing frustration with the virtual straitjacket project was boiling over, and he couldn't let it affect his performance at work or home.

A silhouette of a man appeared in the reflection on John's computer monitor. He closed his eyes and inhaled.

Please don't be Fletcher.

John turned and exhaled. It was Raj.

"Is something wrong, John? You haven't said a word to anyone all day."

John looked around the room and motioned for Raj to lean over.

"I'm working on my virtual straitjacket project at home," John whispered. He scanned the room another time. "It's not working, and it's super frustrating."

"What's it doing?"

John explained his code and all his tests to Raj.

"The code sounds right to me, but let me think about it, and if I think of something else that may work, I'll send it to you."

John swiveled his chair all the way around to face Raj. "I'd appreciate that. I could use a second set of eyes on this project."

Raj opened his mouth to say something but stopped.

"What?" John asked.

"It's nothing. I'll let you know if I come up with something new."

John departed at five o'clock and drove home. He couldn't get the code for his virtual straitjacket out of his mind.

"It should work," John said to himself at a stoplight.

Stacy was preparing to leave as soon as John arrived home.

"I've got to pick up the boys from flag football. Can you watch

CHAPTER 8

Abby, so I don't have to drag her with me?"

"Sure."

John took Abby into his office with him. He put her on his lap while he reread his code for the tenth time.

Abby pointed to the mannequin. "What's that?"

"That's for work, Pumpkin. I need to get its arms to snap back against its body when I push this button, but I can't get it to work. I don't think Daddy will ever launch one of my projects."

Abby jumped off his lap and inspected the stiff nose, lips, and fingers of the plastic person.

"Can you do it now?"

"That's the problem, honey. I can't get it to work. I don't think I can make it do what I want. It may be time for me to stop chasing this dream."

"Just tell your computer to do it."

John laughed and ruffled her hair. "I wish it were that easy."

After reviewing the code one more time, John stood up. "Who's hungry for dinner?"

Abby raised her hand. "Me!"

John took a few steps away from his makeshift desk, and his phone pinged. He walked back to read the message. It was Raj, and he had some new code for him to try. John sat back down and typed in the revised code.

"Daddy, are we going to eat?"

"Just a sec. My friend sent me some help. I have to test this one more time."

After John added the last number to a long string of characters, he closed his eyes and said a silent prayer.

John opened his eyes and clicked submit. Both arms snapped to the side of the worn mannequin. He jumped up with both arms high in the air.

"It worked!"

Abby maintained a blank expression on her face until she saw the mannequin.

"Wahoo!" the youngest Nickerson hooted.

John rushed over to his daughter and picked her up. He spun her around and then set her down. He stared at the code on his screen.

"Of course. I never would've thought of that."

John picked up his phone and typed out a text message to Raj.

Thank you so much for your help. It worked.

John turned to Abby. "I'm going to start a business!"

Chapter 9

Connor caught a pass and ran out of bounds for a first down. The small crowd cheered Connor on for the accomplishment.

Stacy elbowed John. "He caught it and got the first down,"

John looked up from his phone. "That's great."

"Did you even see it?"

"I'm sorry. I was just going over the stuff I need to provide to create a business plan. It sounds like Greek to me."

Stacy stared back with her mouth open. She said nothing and didn't have to.

"I'm putting my phone away now. I won't look at it again during the game."

"Thank you."

Later that evening, John attempted to fill in the questions in the business plan software he purchased.

"Why does this have to be so complicated?" He asked the screen. "I just want to sell a product the public needs. One that can save lives. Why do I need to create a cash flow statement?"

He slammed the laptop shut. He needed to take a break to clear his head. Five minutes later, John found himself a dozen houses from his own. John looked like a typical neighbor going out for a late-night walk, but he was doing so much more. He was trying to process the mountain of information he needed to understand to launch his business.

John stopped at an intersection. Despite the absence of traffic, he stood and waited.

Once John finished his mental construction of the current assets and liabilities of a balance sheet, he crossed the street. He continued his evening stroll. Something caught John's eye, and his pace slowed. Five steps later, he stopped.

He looked at the address on the mailbox and confirmed that he was one lot away from his sister and brother-in-law's house. A white truck had backed into their driveway. He thought he saw a shadow of a man moving in the dark garage.

"I don't think that's Frank's truck," John whispered.

The house was dark except for the foyer light. It was the light Kayla always left on for Kyle so he could come inside under the safety of the light after arriving home late in the evening. She vowed to leave it on forever as a reminder that she'd reunite with her son again in their heavenly home.

A silhouette darted from the garage to the back of the truck. A thud echoed off the metal frame of the truck bed.

John stiffened, and a ball of heat formed in his gut.

"My sister is being robbed!" he hissed to himself.

Fueled by adrenaline, John bent and scurried toward the truck like he was entering a chopper. When he arrived at the end of his sister's driveway, John could see the person picking up boxes in the garage and transferring them to the truck. It was apparent the person was not Frank or Kayla. John assumed it had to be a young person based on the speed the silhouette moved from the garage to the truck.

John looked around. Nobody else was aware of the crime unfolding in the driveway. It was up to him to stop it.

When the person went back into the garage, John pulled out

CHAPTER 9

his phone. He couldn't see the license plate number or confirm the make and model of the truck. John kept the truck between him and the perpetrator.

Once he reached the front of the truck, John bent down and memorized the license plate number. He observed the Toyota logo but wasn't sure of the model.

John asked himself, *Should I call 911 now or get the right model?*

His perfectionism won over, so John sneaked to the back of the truck to find the model. After hearing another thud and a large object sliding forward, he rushed along the passenger side and tried to stick his neck out far enough to see the model on the tailgate. It was too dark.

John turned to head back to the street to call the police when he felt his feet leave the pavement and cool steel press against his back. Next, John heard, "You picked the wrong truck today!"

John raised his arms to defend against any blows. When they didn't come, he confronted the man holding him by the collar and pressing him against the truck.

"I saw what you are doing. I know Frank Rhodes, and you are not him. I'm calling the police."

The man released his grip on John's collar and backed up two steps.

"You know Frank Rhodes? I thought you were trying to steal something from my truck."

"Yes, I know Frank. He's my brother-in-law. Who are you?"

The man opened the passenger door, and the bed light turned on, illuminating the identity of both men.

"I remember you. You were a pallbearer at Kyle's funeral."

"Yes, I was. I'm Kyle's uncle. Why are you sneaking around Frank and Kayla's garage in the dark? What are you putting in your truck?"

The man let out a chuckle. Then his rolling laugh turned into a deep belly laugh. John stood in disbelief at the humor this man found in the situation.

"I'm not sure what is so funny about that."

The man put his hand over his stomach. He caught his breath long enough to respond. "Sorry, I'm laughing because you think I'm stealing from Kyle's parents. I'm Trevor, and I'm picking up some of Kyle's belongings for Mrs. Rhodes. She is donating them to the Wounded Warrior Project."

John furrowed his brow and squinted his eyes. "Why are you doing it in the dark when they aren't home?"

Trevor laughed again. "I guess this looks pretty bad, doesn't it? Mr. and Mrs. Rhodes are at the movies, and she knows I am running a load to the project tomorrow. She texted me their garage door code, and when I got here, their light was burned out. She told me the boxes she wanted to donate were up against the wall, so I thought I'd use the streetlight to load up and get out of here before they came home and found me blocking their garage. I didn't think I'd run into anybody in the five minutes I'd be here."

It was John's turn to chuckle. "I'm sorry, Trevor. I know how much my big sister's family has been through, and the thought of someone stealing from them got my blood boiling. Were you a friend of Kyle?"

Trevor looked down at the ground. His voice cracked when he responded. "Yes, we served together in Mosel, Iraq and hung out after we both came home. He helped me get my business started. I really miss…." Trevor's voice trailed off, and he focused on the pavement again.

"What kind of business do you have?" John asked to shift topics.

CHAPTER 9

Trevor smiled. "I started out installing home entertainment systems, and because of Kyle's help, I started doing smart home installations about a year ago. The business has been booming ever since."

"I can imagine. I work for a commercial security company, and we've been slammed. My plan is to launch a company, but I'm a software engineer, not a businessman, so I'm not sure if I can do it."

"I hear you. I know how to be a field artillery radar operator, not a businessperson. I got help from some retired business owners through the Small Business Administration. Some are even available for hire as consultants."

"Wow, that's exactly what I need. Do you have a contact?"

Trevor reached into his wallet and pulled out his business card.

"Send me an email, and I'll send you contact information for the guy who helped me."

"Absolutely. Thanks so much." John extended his hand and Trevor shook it.

"After I get you the contact information be sure to call him. It will change your business."

Chapter 10

Two days after the misunderstanding in his sister's driveway, John emailed Trevor. He replied ten minutes later with his contact at the Small Business Administration, and John called him later that day.

After a brief conversation on the phone, John set an appointment for a free consultation with the retired business owner. The following week, he entered the compact conference room at the SBA and stopped. The advisor was John in twenty-five years. He was the same height, a few pounds lighter, and had a full head of white hair. He even wore rimless glasses like John.

My twin, John thought. *I only hope I can be as good in business as this guy.*

The start-up business advisor accumulated thirty-six years of experience as a business owner. He started a small tax and accounting firm by himself, and after the first decade, it grew to nine CPAs and two dozen employees until he retired six years ago.

John started the meeting with an overview of his business idea.

"How are you going to fund the business?" the advisor asked John.

"My wife and I have savings set aside to start a business that

I'll use."

"What about after that runs out?"

John stiffened at the question. *How does he know how much I have saved?*

"I guess I wasn't planning to run out. What do you recommend?"

"Mr. Nickerson, hopefully, you will be one of the lucky owners that don't need more than your personal savings, but in all my years in accounting, I haven't seen it happen yet. Do you have friends or family who can lend you money, or do you have equity in your home?"

John crossed his arms and leaned back in his chair. "At some point, I would like to have stock to sell to investors, but I don't have any friends or family I could ask for money right now."

The thought of asking Kayla made his stomach turn sour.

"I do have equity in my house, but I was hoping to get a bank loan instead."

The advisor shuffled some papers. "I can help you get started on the paperwork for a limited liability corporation or LLC so that in the future, you'll have the ability to issue membership units to investors. Further down the road, I'd advise you to get legal counsel on the best tax structure for your business. At this point, you are not going to be able to get a bank loan until you establish creditworthiness for your business, and when you do, the bank will require a personal guarantee with collateral—a home or another asset of value. My advice is to look into a personal home equity loan now so you may be able to avoid the bank loan later."

All of this information was coming at John so fast. He was still processing a potential conversation with Stacy about a home equity loan and didn't respond to the advisor.

"Enough on funding your business. Let's look more closely at the plan you've developed."

The meeting with the advisor lasted several hours. By the end of their consultation, John understood the basics of financial reporting, so the once menacing cash flow statement and balance sheet no longer felt impossible for John.

The advisor tossed him another curveball. He charged John to identify the team that would take his fledgling company from a startup idea to a real revenue-generating business.

"Find people with unique skills and strengths that you don't have," the advisor said.

That would not be easy for John. Most of the people he knew were also software engineers or computer programmers. He'd met other moms and dads of the kids that played on the same sports teams as his boys, but the thought of approaching them about their business skills was daunting.

Once John arrived home, he jotted down a handful of positions and wrote TBD next to them on his yellow legal notepad. He couldn't link a name to a single potential open job title. This new task kept John awake late every night since it was assigned by his advisor. John didn't know how to build a small team for a startup with individuals he knew.

On his commute to work, John talked aloud as he continued to consider his options. "I guess I could go to networking functions. I think the chamber of commerce holds events to help business owners meet."

Still not sold on his solution, he curled his hand into a fist and pounded it on his steering wheel a few times. "That's it! I'll ask people for referrals."

John was sure he found the solution to complete his organizational chart. Referrals would provide qualified candidates

CHAPTER 10

and widen his net of potential people to fill each role.

John readjusted his grip on the steering wheel and stepped on the gas with a little more force than usual after the light turned green.

Later that afternoon, John stopped at Raj's desk to ask him a question about a project they were both working on. After Raj answered, John slipped in his question for a referral.

"Hey Raj, do you know anybody that does marketing on the side or as a freelancer?"

Raj's eyebrows met near his crinkled nose. "Why do you need help with marketing?"

John was so excited to build his list of candidates that he never considered a question from Raj. He stammered, "I — I—my wife said they were looking for one at her office?"

"Why would a dentist need a marketing person? Doesn't Doctor Beasley work off referrals?"

Redness filled John's cheeks as he rubbed the back of his neck. "I don't know. I didn't ask why. I just said I'd help and ask around."

John shifted his weight back and forth as he waited for an answer. Perhaps referrals weren't the solution to his problem.

"No, I don't know anyone in marketing. Most of the people I know are in research and healthcare."

John straightened and fired his next question to Raj the moment he finished. "Do you know someone who does both? Medical research?"

Raj stood up and leaned on the edge of his desk. "What's with all the questions on people I know? What's going on?"

"Nothing is going on. I just want to know." John looked down at his watch. "I've got to get back to my project. Fletcher will be looking for it soon."

"Wait." Raj put up his hand and looked around the office. He waved John to come closer to him and then whispered, "Is this about a new business you are starting?"

John tried to muster the most offended and surprised look possible. "No. No. That's not it at all."

Raj stared into John's eyes until he had to break the stare and look away. Raj stood and took one more step toward John. "Okay, but if you do, don't forget about me. I want in."

Is he serious? Was it a good idea to tell Raj?

"Okay, fine, I'll tell you. Yes, I'm doing some research on what it will take to launch my idea. Nothing is final yet, but I'm trying to find out who can help if I do it."

"Is this the one with the transmitters from Germany?"

"Yeah, I tested it at home, and it works. I need to do more tests. Tests with humans, which is why I asked about medical research. I think it can be a big idea."

Raj nodded. "I thought you were up to something. I can introduce you to my cousin who does the medical research, but I was serious about wanting in."

John looked down at his watch again. "Okay, I need to get back to work before Mr. Fletcher comes looking for me. We can't discuss this at work, so if you are serious, meet me down the street at Hill Country Grille after work, and we can talk about it."

Raj clenched his jaw. "I'm serious."

Chapter 11

Once John's eyes adjusted to the indoor light, he scanned the patrons inside Hill Country Grille but didn't see Raj. He saw a co-worker from Fletcher Security sitting at the bar. Eric from Finance sat behind a mug of beer with two friends. John considered aborting the mission, but he didn't know Eric very well. Plus, he didn't think Eric saw him.

John moved behind the divider between the bar and dining room to stay out of Eric's line of sight. He scanned the room again and still didn't see Raj. Maybe Raj wasn't serious after all.

John walked deeper into the dining room and saw Raj scrolling through his phone at a high-top table.

"Hey Raj, I'm glad you came. I wasn't sure if you were serious."

"Yes, I am serious. Tell me more about your idea."

John jerked his head toward the bar, "We have company from Fletcher, so we've got to keep this quiet."

Raj looked toward the bar and nodded after he saw Eric.

For the next ten minutes, John explained the results of his tests and the plan to launch his concept as the flagship product of his new company. Raj never said a word the entire time. He nodded and jotted down notes.

"So, what do you think? Do you like the product concept and the business plan?"

Raj took a drink of sweet tea.

"Yeah, I think you are on the right track, but you will have to do more testing to get large, established companies to pay for it. Have you tested it on anything else but the mannequin?"

"No, not yet. That is why I asked you about the medical researcher. I need an economical way to test my virtual straitjacket concept on humans. No organization will pay for it without credible test data on people."

Raj wrote down several lines of notes. He put the pen down and looked across the table at John. "I may have a good option. My cousin Sanjay works in the research lab at a medical assistant school out by the airport. Sometimes they let the public come in so they can experience working on actual patients. Other times they pay citizens to be actors and pretend to have certain injuries or illnesses so the students can get practice diagnosing patients. They pay a hundred dollars for one hour, so one time I volunteered to be a patient, and they gave me an index card that said 'concussion' and several symptoms for me to pretend I had. It took three students almost the full hour to diagnose me. One student recommended that they should transfer me to social services for a psychiatric evaluation. She thought I was crazy. It was the most accurate diagnosis of me yet."

Raj let out an obnoxious laugh. He grabbed the round table with one hand and slapped the top with his other hand as his laughter grew louder.

John let out a courtesy chuckle and then waited for Raj to compose himself. "Interesting story, Raj, but how does that apply to me?"

Raj stopped laughing and straightened up. "Oh yeah, for some items, they use the students to conduct the tests. Students were

CHAPTER 11

testing safety shields and goggles from a new vendor the day I was there. They had a sign-up sheet on the wall for students to test a new blood pressure monitor, so I know they'll test new products. I'm sure it has a cost, but I don't know how much."

John stroked at the two-day-old stubble on his chin. "Sounds promising. Can you get more information from your cousin?"

"Sure, I'll call him on the way home."

John stood up and pushed in his chair. "Thanks for your help, Raj."

"You bet. Like I said, I want in."

Two hours later, John received a text from Raj. It said the school charged $250 per student to conduct research in their facility—half went to the school and the other half to the students.

John put the phone down on the coffee table and leaned back on his couch. He sunk into the deep cushions as he estimated the number of students he would have to test. Twenty was his first estimate, but five thousand dollars was far more than he felt comfortable spending.

John wondered if he should investigate the home equity loan further at this time. He leaned forward and put his face into his cupped hands. He raked his fingers through his hair and sat back up.

"I'll just have to test fewer students," John said aloud.

Ten students would work. John told himself that it was double digits, so it was much better than testing nine or fewer students. It would look better on their sell sheet to future prospects.

John texted Raj back. *Tell your cousin we'd like to test 10 students. Let us know how soon we can conduct the test.*

Two weeks later, John and Raj left Fletcher Security after their workday ended and arrived in the lobby of the medical assistant school a few minutes before their six o'clock appointment. Moments after the front desk attendant notified Sanjay that his clients were in the lobby, he burst through the double doors with a smile. He looked like Raj's taller twin in navy blue scrubs and white Nike running shoes.

Sanjay shook hands with John and then escorted both men back to the test room. He went over the test guidelines and protocols.

"How many students do you plan to test today?"

John cleared his throat. "It will take some time to hook up every student with the transmitters, so I'd like to do five today and the remaining five tomorrow."

"Okay. I'll let you set up, and I'll send the first student in ten minutes."

The first student arrived. It was a woman in her late thirties going back to school after her youngest child started first grade. "So, what are you going to be testing on me?"

John delivered the best reassuring smile he could conjure. He held up a transmitter so the student could see it clearly. "I'll glue these transmitters to your skin with this medical-grade adhesive to four places on your body. I'll apply them to your elbow and forearm areas on each arm. Last, I will tape this microprocessor to your hip. When I activate the transmitters on my laptop, your arms will tighten up against your body until I deactivate them."

The student's forehead developed several rows of wrinkles. "What product are you testing?"

"This is a new and improved containment system for law enforcement."

The student stared back at John.

CHAPTER 11

"They are like better handcuffs for the police."

"Oh, okay," the student replied as the wrinkles on her forehead smoothed out.

"Any more questions?"

"Will it hurt?"

"No, not one bit."

The student exhaled, and John glued the transmitters to the student. He finished fifteen minutes later and turned to Raj. He was sitting at a nearby desk behind a laptop.

"Is the code ready?"

Raj squinted at the screen and looked back up at John. "It's ready."

"Good. On the count of three, please activate the virtual straitjacket."

"The what?" The student inquired with a look of alarm, but John was already in his countdown.

"Two, three, activate!"

Raj clicked his mouse, and the student's arms rushed to her sides.

"How does it feel? Are you in any pain?"

"No pain. I feel like someone behind me put me in a big hug. I can't move my arms."

John smiled. "Raj, please deactivate."

A moment later, the student's arms moved away from her torso. She shook them out and turned to John. "It wasn't too bad. I guess it worked."

"Yes, it did. Do you have any other feedback for us before you leave?"

"Yeah, get a better name."

The student left, and John walked over to Raj. He held up his hand for a high five.

"It worked, buddy. This is looking like the real deal."

The next two students had similar results. John's confidence in his first human prototypes grew with each successful test.

The fourth student was a young lady who just transferred to the medical assistant school after first attending a dental hygienist school. She was a long-distance runner, and John had trouble getting the transmitters to stick to the lean muscles in her arms. It took a few more minutes, but soon John had all four transmitters ready to test.

The countdown started, and her arms clung to her sides once activated like the previous three students, but before John could ask a question, something went wrong. Her left forearm and right elbow pulled away from her body. The sound of two tiny metallic objects hitting the floor drew the attention of John, Raj, and the student.

"They popped off," Raj said.

John bent down to examine her arms.

"Sure did."

John removed the remaining transmitters and thanked the student for her time. He placed the transmitters on the tray next to the test subject chair. "I'll have to be more careful with the glue next time."

The last student for the evening was a youthful man fresh out of junior college. He was new to the medical assistant school and was four months away from his twentieth birthday. John glued the transmitters to his arms and began his countdown as he did with the previous four students.

"One, two, three, activate."

John watched as two arms whipped in front of his face. The student's arms crossed his chest like a real straitjacket, and he yelped in pain. "Ouch. This hurts. Please turn it off."

CHAPTER 11

The student panicked. He tried to wiggle free from the virtual straight jacket and fell to the floor. He screamed as if his life was in grave danger. "Turn it off! Turn it off!"

John turned to Raj. His mouth was frozen open as he watched the student writhe in pain. He jumped over the student and hit the deactivate button.

"What's going on?" Sanjay shouted as he burst through the door.

Sanjay looked down and saw the student on the white and gray tile floor. He arrived next to the student at the same time as John.

"Are you okay?" John asked.

"Get me out of here!"

The student pushed away at John's hands, checked his extremities for injuries, and then jumped to his feet. He dug at the transmitter adhesive with his fingers. Seconds later, he removed the fourth transmitter and threw it at John.

"Take that. You said it wasn't painful. I thought I could die."

The student stomped to the door and slammed it behind him.

John saw the look of disappointment on Sanjay's face.

"What happened, Raj? John? Somebody say something!"

"I think I may have mixed up the transmitters after they fell off the last student. I must have put the right elbow on his left forearm."

Sanjay turned red. "That's unacceptable and inexcusable. That goes against every protocol we discussed two hours ago. I could get written up for this."

John put his hands in his pockets and stared at the floor. "I'm sorry. I won't let it happen again."

"No, you won't because that was your last test in this school. Please pack up your stuff and leave."

Raj spoke for the first time since he froze. "Sanjay, please don't—"

"I'm even more disappointed in you. I believed you when you said your friend had a wonderful product that needed to conduct final human tests. This product isn't even close to being ready for human testing. You conned me."

Sanjay's comments played in John's mind the rest of the night. He knew he was even further away now than he was before the test. Was this the last nail in the virtual straitjacket coffin?

Chapter 12

The next day, neither John nor Raj mentioned the incident at the medical assistant school. John didn't sleep at all, and based on the dark circles under Raj's eyes, he suffered the same fate.

John buried himself in his work at the office and then at home during the weekend to keep his mind off the virtual straitjacket project. It was too painful to recall the incident with the student or acknowledge the lack of opportunities to conduct tests on humans.

Monday afternoon, while John filled his screen with new code, a familiar voice interrupted him. It was Raj.

"I talked to Sanjay this weekend."

John looked around the room to ensure nobody else could hear their conversation. "Was he still mad?"

"He didn't get written up, so he's not as angry now."

"Good. Do you think he'll let us test his students again?"

"Oh, no. Sanjay said he'd never let me or anyone I recommend inside his facility ever again."

John let his head drop.

"It wasn't all terrible news, though."

John looked up. "Okay, I'm not sure what positive news could have come out of last week."

"Sanjay said he likes your concept, but that you are doing it all wrong."

"I'm listening."

"He said you must embed the transmitters under the skin to ensure they stay in place in the right location. Sanjay said he sees medical devices inserted just under the skin all the time."

John pursed his lips and nodded.

"He also said you should add a transmitter to each hand near the thumb if you want to subdue a person properly. If someone can still move their hands, they can still grab you or even a weapon. Transmitters in the elbows, forearm, and hand will give you absolute command over the individual."

Raj finished sharing Sanjay's recommendation, and John stared through him at a blank wall. Raj turned to make sure nobody else was coming and then back to John. "So, what do you think?"

"It makes complete sense. I wasn't sure how to secure the transmitters to a person with an adhesive, and I never considered inserting them under the skin. That could solve several problems."

A faint smile crept across John's face then vanished.

"Do you think Sanjay would show me how to purchase the correct medical equipment and then how to insert the transmitters under a person's skin the proper way?"

Raj looked like John asked him to feed a wild grizzly bear. "I'm not sure that is a good idea right now."

"Can you give him a few more days to cool down and then ask?"

"Okay, I'll ask him next week."

Just as Raj and John were ending their discussion, Karl Fletcher entered the room with Eric from Finance. Although Eric was an assistant manager in his early thirties, Mr. Fletcher included him in most projects over the director of finance. John assumed it was because Eric looked more like a bodyguard than a numbers geek. Eric was a half foot taller than Mr. Fletcher and looked like he could be featured on the cover of a Scottish rugby magazine. John thought Mr. Fletcher puffed out his chest a bit more when Eric was by his side.

Ray scurried back to his desk. John tapped his keyboard in a frenzy to ensure several lines of code were visible when Mr. Fletcher stopped by to check on him. Mr. Fletcher didn't stop. He passed by in a rush and continued down the hall. It appeared as if the CEO was planning a surprise attack on someone else in operations.

Eric followed Mr. Fletcher step by step. John turned in his chair to verify that the threat left the engineering room and saw Eric turn around and look back. He gave John a side-eye that sent a quick burst of adrenaline in his stomach. John felt like Eric had yelled out, "I see what you are doing," but he never said a word. He didn't have to.

John turned to Raj to see if he saw the same thing. He raised both hands with palms up toward Raj. Raj shrugged his shoulders and pivoted back to his computer monitor. He must have felt Eric's glare as well.

Rumors circulated the office several months ago that Eric was doing the dirty work for Mr. Fletcher with employees who had crossed the company founder. John was sure he was on Mr. Fletcher's hit list but figured he could avoid him. Eric was nimbler in the office and harder to avoid.

Was Eric a threat to take down John and his dream?

Chapter 13

"He said, yes!" Raj was beaming with excitement as he approached John in the parking lot.

They both turned toward the Fletcher Security building and sauntered to the entrance to start their day.

"Sanjay said he'll help. He said he'll teach you what to use and how to do it; that's it. He doesn't want to be around when you test anyone again, but he'll help teach you."

John stopped to face Raj. His lips curled up, and he extended his fist, and Raj returned the bump. "That's awesome. Thanks for all your help on this, Raj."

They reached the front entrance, and John pulled open one of the double doors. "After you."

Raj took two steps and stopped in the doorway.

John leaned his head around the heavily tinted door and saw the reason Raj stopped.

Eric was standing in front of him with his hands on his hips.

John curled around the door.

"Go ahead, Raj. I'm coming in."

Eric turned to the side and let both men pass him. Just as John picked up his pace, he heard Eric speak.

"What are you two up to?"

John shot a glance at Raj to tell him he'd take this question.

CHAPTER 13

"Nothing. Just heading to our desks."

"No, it's more than that. I've been watching you two."

John felt the hair on the back of his neck stand up. He cleared his throat. "What do you mean?"

"You two are planning something. I see you whispering in the office and sneaking around after work to collude about something."

John's legs turned weak, and he wobbled in the shadow of Eric the Great. He caught a quick glimpse of Raj. John had never seen his face so pale.

"Can't two friends hang out after work?"

"Yeah, I'm not buying that. I think you two are planning to start a new business or something."

John raised his hand in a stop position. "No, no, it's nothing like—"

"I know the signs, guys. I've been doing it myself with some of my college friends after work. That's when I saw you two at the Hill Country Grille."

Now it was John's turned to be confused.

"You're trying to start your own business?" John squeaked.

"We're trying to do something together, but they're pretty clueless. That's when I thought of you two."

John couldn't speak, and Raj seemed to freeze like he did during the botched test at the medical school.

"I know you two are smart guys, and I thought I'd see if you can cut me in on what you are doing. It has to be better than anything my friends could come up with."

A slew of questions slammed inside John's head. *Was this a trap? Was it a set up to get him to admit he was considering a new business? Was he safe from Eric turning him into Mr. Fletcher?*

"You're trying to start a new business yourself?" John asked.

"Yeah, I've got to get out of this place."

"I thought you were tight with Mr. Fletcher."

Eric laughed a sinister laugh. "That clown? No way. That guy parades me around like I'm one of his henchmen to intimidate everyone. It feels like high school again with him, and I can't take it much longer. What are you two planning?"

John considered telling his new ally but looked over to Raj first. He was shaking his head.

"I don't want to talk about it here. Are you open to meeting after work at that same Hill Country Grille?"

"I'll see you there."

Eric turned and walked toward the finance department.

John and Raj resumed their journey to the software engineering office.

"What just happened?" Raj asked.

"I think we may have just picked up a new partner."

"Are you going to meet him and share our plans?"

"I think it's our only option. Eric is either telling the truth and wants in on our plan, or he's caught on to us and will rat us out to Fletcher soon anyway."

"Okay, but I'm not going tonight."

"That's fine. I'll meet him and share our plans."

Eric was waiting for John just as he promised. John concluded Eric wanted in on their business plan or at least really wanted to leave Fletcher Security, so he shared everything with Eric.

"What do you think?" John asked.

"I like it. I think it has real potential."

"So, how do you want to be involved?"

"I want to get in on something like this early. I want some type of ownership like shares or a percentage of the company."

John smiled. "I am interested in the same thing, but first we need to build the company so we have something to split. Raj and I agreed to work on this without getting paid until we have some business income to divide. At that time, we'll discuss a way to distribute ownership of the company in a way that's fair to everyone. Does that work for you?"

Eric extended his hand to John.

By the end of the dinner, the team grew to three.

Two weeks later, John unfolded three chairs in his home lab. Raj, Eric, and Sanjay would be there in minutes.

Eric arrived first, and then Raj and Sanjay came into the lab. Sanjay brought the kit of three syringes with a dozen twelve-gauge needles he purchased for John and set it on the plywood.

"Is that it?" John asked.

"I also have some topical anesthesia and alcohol wipes. Did you get the sterilized transmitter chips?"

John held up a clear one-gallon zip-lock bag full of smaller packages in silver, metallic pouches. "Yes, they sent them overnight, and I received them yesterday."

"Okay, let me show you how it works and where I recommend you place the transmitters in each person for optimal performance," Sanjay announced.

The four men gathered around the makeshift workstation for the next forty minutes. Once Sanjay finished, Raj spoke first.

"Now, we need to test it on some people."

Sanjay shot him a look.

"I know. None of your students, but we need to test them on people."

John tapped his index finger on his lips. "I don't think I can afford the liability insurance and research fees to run a real clinical trial. We need to find another way to test people."

"I'll do it."

Everyone turned and looked at Eric. The newest member of the team was volunteering to be the first test subject.

"I appreciate the offer, Eric, but I can't let you do it. We need to find another way."

"Why not? If it works like you say it will, I'm okay if you test it on me."

"It's just not right for me to test it on you first. If we test it on any of us, it should be me."

The room went silent. John let the words he uttered sink it. Was he prepared to insert transmitters under his skin to test his concept?

"Nah, you can't do it either. You're the boss," Eric chimed in.

John ran his fingers through his wavy hair as he paced in the tight space. He arrived back at the plywood table in the lab.

"Sanjay, can you insert two transmitters into my legs?"

He tilted his head and then nodded. "Yeah, I can do it."

"Great! Eric and Raj, let's move some boxes so we can get a chair set up by the wall. I'll be right back."

"Where are you going?" Eric asked.

"I'm changing into shorts. We are testing this on me tonight."

Chapter 14

The size of the needle to insert the transmitters was fatter and longer than John expected. He was sure his eyes looked like small blue marbles in the center of white dinner plates when Sanjay pulled it out of the medical bag.

Sanjay put on latex gloves and wiped the target area on John's leg with an alcohol pad. "Remember to always sanitize with an alcohol wipe first, then add a bead of the 4% lidocaine cream to help numb the area a bit. The twelve-millimeter chip requires a larger needle than most people are used to at the doctor's office, so the lidocaine helps. The tube I brought with me is from the medical supply distributor, but you can buy the same strength at any drug store."

Sanjay waited a minute for the lidocaine to kick in and secured John's skin above the inside of his right knee and removed the cream residue with another alcohol wipe. He readjusted his grip until he found a spot he liked and then held it with this index finger and thumb.

Sanjay shared with the onlookers. "I'd say right about there. You want the meaty part of the quad on the inside of the knee."

Sanjay moved the needle closer to John.

He tightened all his muscles in his legs and his butt until he was no longer even touching the chair.

"I need to get some skin, and it's hard when your muscle is tense like that."

"Sorry, but it looks like it will hurt," John replied through gritted teeth.

"Relax. Let the anesthetic do its job."

John closed his eyes and bowed his head. He asked Jesus to keep them safe and guide Sanjay's needle into the right position. John opened his eyes. He exhaled and turned his head. "Okay, I'm ready now. Hurry up and do it before I change my mind."

"Enter at a forty-five-degree angle and make sure the beveled part of the needle is facing up as you insert it under the skin," Sanjay said slowly as he inserted the needle.

John felt the pressure of the needle and then a quick stinging sensation once it penetrated the skin. It was similar to a shot from the dentist after they pre-applied lidocaine. A brief moment of discomfort but limited pain.

"Be sure to press the plunger all the way down to ensure you clear the chip from the needle."

John turned his head back to see Sanjay pulling the needle out from under his skin.

"Apply pressure to the injection site using your finger as you withdraw the needle and gently massage the area."

Sanjay put a piece of gauze over the injection site and secured it with a piece of first-aid tape.

"Now that wasn't so bad, was it?" Sanjay asked with a grin.

"No, it wasn't as bad as I thought it would be."

"You may feel a small lump for another day or two at the injection site and that is normal. Are you ready for chip number two now?" Sanjay asked.

The men finished inserting the rest of the chips into John's legs and were ready for the critical test of the transmitters. John remained in the chair while Eric taped the master transmitter to his waist, and Raj completed the code on the laptop.

Raj looked up. "It's ready."

Eric widened his stance next to John to help catch him if he lurched forward.

"Countdown from three, Raj, when you are ready," John said in a shaky voice.

Raj tapped the keyboard a few more times. "Okay, three, two, one, activate."

All eyes turned to John. He held tightly to the armrests, but nothing happened.

"Are you serious?" John said while shaking his head.

"Wait. Oops. Let's try this again."

Raj hit activate again without a countdown, and John was not ready.

John's legs slammed together at his knees, and he fell backward and hit his head on the wall. Eric moved closer with his arms outstretched, but John stayed in the chair. He checked the back of his head with his fingers, and it was only a minor bump.

Moments later, Raj, Sanjay, and Eric surrounded John.

"How does it feel?" Raj asked.

"It feels like I have a belt wrapped around my knees. It's a little uncomfortable, but it doesn't hurt. I can't pull them apart at all. Deactivate it now, Raj."

Raj walked back to the laptop and tapped a key. John's legs separated and smiles stretched across all their faces.

"It works!" Eric cried with a pump of his fist.

John shook his legs and rubbed them once with his hands. "Let's do it again, Raj and this time with a countdown."

They tested John's leg transmitters three times. All the tests were successful, so they made plans to advance their testing. Eric was adamant that he would be next. He would be the test dummy for the complete test in the arms and legs.

For the rest of the evening, the men tested the transmitters on Eric. They worked every time.

John addressed the team. "Thank all of you for your help tonight."

"What do we test next?" Eric inquired.

John did not respond. He was mentally adding the costs of the transmitters he already purchased, the new transmitters he needed to buy, legal fees to file a patent, additional test fees and everything else that was pushing him toward a home equity loan. He wasn't ready for that conversation with Stacy yet.

Eric looked around the room and walked toward John until he was right in front of him. "Earth to John, what do we test next?"

"Oh, sorry. We test the business."

"The business?"

"Yes, we need to get a proposal in front of a potential customer and see what they say."

Eric and Raj looked at each other. "Do you want to tell him?" Raj asked Eric.

"Tell me what?"

Eric cleared his throat. "If we are going to present this to customers, we need a better name. The business needs a name. Virtual straitjacket is horrible."

John put his hands up in surrender and laughed. "Okay, I agree. I haven't spent too much time on the name because I wasn't sure I'd need to. Let's all brainstorm some ideas, and we can decide next time we meet."

John locked the door behind the last person to leave. He fell

CHAPTER 14

back against the door and looked up to heaven. "Thank you."

Chapter 15

"He went to his car, and when he returned, he gunned down all three men inside," blared the TV. John looked up and saw the local evening news anchor on a split-screen with a field reporter.

Stacy sat on the couch with a magazine and a bowl of popcorn beside her.

"How can you watch this?"

Stacy looked up from her magazine. "Watch what?"

"The news. Or should I say the bad news?"

Stacy raised the magazine off her lap. "I'm not paying attention, but I want to hear the sports and weather when that comes on."

John sat down in the empty cushion on the other side of the popcorn bowl. He popped a few fluffy white kernels in his mouth.

"How were the kids tonight?"

"They were fine. A few dust-ups like we have every day, but not too bad. How did your meeting with the guys go for your straitjacket project?"

John straightened up and smiled. "It went great. Every test worked, so we are ready to show it to potential customers."

"What happened to your legs?" Stacy asked as she pointed to

CHAPTER 15

the bright red marks on John's inner leg.

"Oh yeah. We're inserting the transmitters under the skin now. They are far more reliable and work much better under the skin."

"So, you let them test the transmitters under your skin?"

"Eric did it too," John replied, sounding like a fifth grader tattling to his teacher.

Stacy shook her head.

"What?"

"Nothing."

"Why are you shaking your head?"

"I don't know how you will get many companies to sign up for a product that requires them to insert chips under their skin. Have you thought at all about that?"

The honest answer was that he had not, and John sensed Stacy knew that. She knew that John liked to follow his ideas on pure hope and adrenaline. She was the voice of reason that considered all the possibilities of John's ideas, including losing the house and cars.

"You're starting to sound like the guys now."

"Oh, did one of them point out the possibility that most people don't want to shoot electronic doohickeys under their skin?"

"No, they all saw how well it worked, so they like the product concept. They don't like my product name. They said Virtual Straitjacket was a horrible name."

Stacy stared at John for several seconds before responding. "I was hoping for a voice of reason in your new band of brothers, but I guess a new name is a good start."

"You don't like the name either?"

Stacy picked up the popcorn bowl and moved toward the

kitchen. Before she vanished into the other room, she stopped and turned back to John. "The guys are right. It makes me think of *One Flew Over the Cuckoo's Nest* every time you say the name. I don't like it."

At bedtime, John laid his head back on the pillow and pulled the comforter up to his chest. He thought about the successful tests and the potential customers who would appreciate their novel technology. John tried to picture the perfect name and logo on the blank canvas in front of him. He woke up the next morning with no suggestions.

Two days later, Raj, Eric, and John chose a booth in the dining room at the Hill Country Grille. The dinner crowd hadn't arrived yet, and the three men wanted to complete their new product and company names before the noise level rose in the room.

Raj was the first to offer a new product name. "How about Python? It works just as well, but without having to carry around a deadly reptile."

John nodded. "Not bad. We'll pass on your descriptive tagline, but not bad for a product name."

"What about Big Bear Hug?" Eric asked with a wide smile.

Raj threw a jalapeno popper across the table and hit Eric in the chest.

"What's that for? If I get you in a bear hug, you ain't going anywhere."

The budding entrepreneurs tossed out a half dozen more names, but none resonated with John. The group turned silent as they all tried to come up with more suggestions.

Raj broke the silence. "How about Sure Cuffs? It explains what it does and should appeal to the target customer who understands that existing restraints are not always reliable."

CHAPTER 15

Eric picked up a fried cheese stick to retaliate against Raj, but John put his hand up to stop him.

"That's not bad, Raj."

John fixed his gaze above Eric's blond locks on the posters on the restaurant walls. He could picture the Sure Cuffs logo on the opening slide of his first presentation. It was descriptive and catchy.

"I love it, Raj."

Raj returned a toothy smile and stuck his neck out to further taunt Eric.

"I'll admit, it's not bad," Eric said, "but what about the company name?"

The table grew quiet again. This time John offered a suggestion.

"I've been thinking about this one for a while. I want a name the gives us the latitude to do a wide range of security-based products. What do you two think about Sectronix as the company name?"

Raj and Eric shot glances at each other. It reminded John of the look he saw in his house the day they told him they hated the virtual straitjacket name.

"So, we'd be offering Sure Cuffs from Sectronix?" Eric asked.

John nodded. "Yes, I guess that's what we'd offer."

Eric smiled. "I love it."

"Me too," Raj chirped.

John raised his glass to the center of the table. "Gentleman, welcome to Sectronix and our breakthrough Sure Cuffs product."

Glasses clinked, and over dinner they each shared their vision for the inevitable success they pictured for their new enterprise.

They were all mistaken.

Chapter 16

Stacy had to work late, so John took the kids to a local park. While he monitored all three kids as they played on the swings and climbed a metal structure that looked like the skeleton of a small skyscraper, John was also thinking about the future of Sectronix. He needed to present Sure Cuffs to a potential client soon so he could understand if it was time to order more transmitters from the German supplier or if he had to conduct more testing.

John considered all the possibilities of the organizations that could benefit from Sure Cuffs. In his mind, he thought every law-enforcement institution should be loyal customers of Sure Cuffs.

After an hour in the park, the shadows engulfed all the playground equipment, and John was ready to take the kids home for dinner. John looked up and saw an older and larger boy pushing Zach away from the merry-go-round full of giggling preteens. Every time Zach would try to get on the spinning roundabout, the larger boy would drive him back with his forearm and then laugh at him. John stood up to intervene but didn't have to. Connor maneuvered his way over the bars and sat next to the larger boy. The next time he tried to push Zach away, Connor leaned into the older boy with all of his

CHAPTER 16

one hundred and twenty pounds. The bully had to pull his arm back to keep from flying off the spinning tempest, and that was all Zach needed. He jumped on the merry-go-round and joined the rest of the kids in laughter. John exhaled and waved to Zach and Connor. He let them enjoy their hard-fought right to ride the merry-go-round a few more minutes before leaving.

During the drive home, they passed his big sister's house. It reminded John of that fateful day when the inmate escaped from the municipal court building in downtown Austin and killed his nephew, Kyle. A pit formed in John's gut as he recalled the event that changed the lives of his whole extended family forever. He pictured the scene on the evening news with the reporter in front of the municipal courthouse in downtown Austin where the inmate escaped.

"That's it. The municipal court building," John whispered to himself.

"What did you say, Daddy?" asked Abby from her car seat.

"Oh, nothing. I just got a brilliant idea."

John arrived home, and Stacy was putting the finishing touches on dinner. He rushed to his lab and opened his laptop. He searched Google and found the head of security at the municipal courthouse in downtown Austin.

"Greg Hopkins. You will be my first customer. You just don't know it yet."

The next day, John called Mr. Hopkins from his SUV during a quick break. The call went into voicemail. After hanging up on his introductory message six times in 24 hours, John left Mr. Hopkins a voicemail after concluding he would never answer his phone.

Two days later, John left Mr. Hopkins a second voicemail. He was getting concerned that the head of security at the municipal courthouse wasn't open to talking to anybody about new security products.

John, Raj, and Eric started meeting at the Hill Country Grille after work every Tuesday. Eric and Raj wanted an updated on Sectronix and Sure Cuffs after the successful test the previous week.

"Have you set up any presentations for Sure Cuffs yet?" Raj asked.

"Not yet. I'm cold calling accounts and leaving voicemails, but so far, nobody will pick up the phone or return a message."

Eric put his elbows on the table and leaned halfway over. John and Raj were on the other side of the table. "Do you know what you need to do now?"

"Keep calling more people?" John asked.

"No. You need to be more aggressive with your target accounts. Wait for them in the lobby or meet them in the parking lot. When you find them, you give them your elevator pitch and then your business card. They'll appreciate your persistence and invite you to deliver a full presentation."

John stared across the table at Eric. He thought that might be a suitable method for Eric and his larger-than-life personality, but John wasn't comfortable being that aggressive.

"I don't know, Eric. That may get a little too pushy. I don't buy from people who are pushy with me."

Eric grew more animated. "No. It's not like that at all. If you have a polished elevator pitch and share it with a prospect, they will think you're confident in your product and will want to learn more about it."

John turned to Raj, who was sitting to his left in the booth. Raj pursed his lips and nodded.

"Yeah, I guess that may work."

CHAPTER 16

"I can do it if you don't want to," Eric replied.

John put up his hand. "No, that won't be necessary. I've been working on an elevator pitch that I can use. Plus, I've been leaving the head of security voicemails at the municipal courthouse in downtown Austin for the past week. He won't return my calls, so I guess it's time to pay him a visit."

Chapter 17

John went home and did more research on Greg Hopkins. He studied his appearance and found out some information on his background. After an hour, John was ready for his ambush presentation to Mr. Hopkins in the parking lot of the municipal courthouse in downtown Austin.

The first day John pulled into the parking lot of the courthouse and gasped at the sight of hundreds of people leaving the building at five o'clock. He stood next to his car to see if he could see Mr. Hopkins but didn't see a man that resembled the picture John had of him.

The next day John walked up to the doors of the courthouse and stopped before he reached the security checkpoint and metal detectors. He moved to the side at five o'clock, and for the next fifteen minutes, he studied every face that left the building toward the employee parking lot. Just when he was ready to give up, John saw a face that matched the one he'd been studying online the past week. John straightened up and tugged at his suit jacket. He took two steps toward Mr. Hopkins and stopped. John hadn't built up enough courage to approach him just yet.

That night, John went home and did more research on Mr. Hopkins to find a personal connection he could use. He scoured social media sites for the right Greg Hopkins until he found the correct profile. A few seconds later, he pumped his fist.

"That's it. He went to Texas State."

On John's third attempt to pitch Greg Hopkins, he was beaming with confidence. He parked his car and marched up to the doors outside security. Twenty minutes after five, he saw the familiar man bounding down the stairs. John made his move.

John approached Greg from his two o'clock position. When he was within five feet, John said, "Go Bobcats."

The man stopped just before he reached the end of the sidewalk.

It worked!

"You from Texas State?"

"My wife went there. We met her junior year, so I spent a lot of time on campus down in San Marcos."

"How did you know I'm from Texas State?"

John cleared his throat and extended his hand with his business card. "I've done my research because I want to share a new product solution that may benefit you."

Mr. Hopkins examined the card. "John Nickerson from Sectronix. Never heard of you."

"We are a startup with a first of its kind product line."

Mr. Hopkins put the card in his pocket and began walking toward his car in the parking lot. John turned and walked shoulder to shoulder with him.

"The product is Sure Cuffs, and it can provide complete control of any inmate under your custody."

The head of security increased his pace.

John pulled a transmitter out of his pocket and held it between his index finger and thumb. "We are the first company to get this breakthrough technology to secure an inmate electronically."

Greg Hopkins arrived at his car and opened the door. Before he could slide in, John raised the transmitter to his eye level so Mr. Hopkins could see it.

"I've seen those before. Another guy showed them to me a few months ago. He said something about securing all our physical files and assets with self-closing doors. I thought you said you were the first company to get this technology."

Heat shot up John's spine like a wildfire. Beads of sweat formed on his forehead. He tried to summon a response, but was mute. He stared at Mr. Hopkins, hoping for a divine intervention of wisdom or at least a coherent response.

"Well. Um, I—" John tried to refute Mr. Hopkins, but couldn't find the words.

Mr. Hopkins closed his door and rolled down the window. He pulled John's card out of his front pocket and looked up at John, standing outside his window like a wounded puppy.

"John, I'll tell you what I told the other guy. I'm not interested in self-closing doors. You should also have your story straight if you want to pitch a new product to me, especially if you want to engage me in the parking lot on the way to my son's soccer practice. Good day, sir."

The tinted window rolled up, and the car backed out of the parking spot. John watched in silence as the black Chrysler sped away.

John shook his head and staggered back to his truck.

I can't believe I froze like that. I had to show him how Sure Cuffs could help him secure his inmates or avoid escapees and I failed.

How severe was this blunder? Did he hurt his chances of ever presenting Sure Cuffs to this high-potential client?

CHAPTER 17

He just hoped it wasn't a fatal mistake.

Chapter 18

John couldn't get the encounter with Greg Hopkins out of his mind. He tossed and turned all night and slept less than three hours.

It was Saturday, and John was already dreading going into work on Monday. He knew Raj and Eric would want an immediate update on his parking-lot pitch, but it was a challenge to relive that painful encounter. John was embarrassed that he didn't consider a member of the Fletcher Security sales team, known for pushing new products faster than the competition, might have already shown the transmitters to large, local customers. It explained why Mr. Fletcher was so negative about the technology—he must've heard from the sales team how quickly the courthouse dismissed the product.

John got dressed, splashed water on his face and looked in the mirror. "I'm not sure a startup is for me. No wonder so many businesses fail their first year."

He joined his family in the kitchen. Stacy had just set down a plate full of French toast and turkey sausage in front of the kids, so they were quiet. John filled his cup with coffee and leaned against the counter. He stared out the window above the kitchen sink at the oak leaves swaying in the wind.

"You seem quiet today. What's wrong?" Stacy asked.

CHAPTER 18

"Nothing is wrong. I've just got a lot on my mind."

"The French toast will occupy the kids for a few minutes, so you may as well tell me now."

John stared into Stacy's green eyes. She was his biggest supporter, but he hated to disappoint her more than anyone else. He exhaled and told her about Greg Hopkins.

The look on Stacy's face after John shared the story told him all he needed to know about his mistake. She knew it was a doozy.

"Wow, that had to sting."

"It did. It's pretty frustrating and humbling to have that happen on your first sales attempt."

"What are you going to do about work?"

John tilted his head. "What do you mean?"

"Aren't you worried that the guy at the courthouse will tell somebody at Fletcher Security about you?"

John's stomach lurched, and for a moment, he felt like he was free falling. Despite laying awake most of the night, he never considered that possibility. He was so concerned with the missed opportunity with Sectronix that he failed to see the potential damaging outcome at his current job. *Another rookie move*, he thought.

"I don't think he would say anything. He doesn't know where I work or who I am, so he wouldn't do that."

"I thought you said you gave him a Sectronix business card with your name on it."

"I did, but he doesn't know where I work."

"Yeah, but he could find out the other company that presented the transmitter to him if he wanted to."

John stormed out of the kitchen. "I know I made a mistake. I don't want to rehash it over and over."

He slammed the door to his lab and put his coffee on the plywood table. John pounded his fist on the table, and droplets of coffee flew out of the cup onto his workstation.

The lab door opened, and Stacy stuck her head inside.

"Can I come in?"

John nodded.

"I'm not trying to pile on, but I think it's a possibility this guy could tell someone, and you should be prepared for it."

"What do you think I should do?" John whispered.

"I think you need to be honest and upfront with Mr. Fletcher. You should go to him first and tell him you made a mistake. Explain that you got excited about your idea and wanted to see if you could get a customer interested to help support your idea, but it didn't work. Now you understand your mistake and will drop the idea for good this time."

"That's not true, though."

"It's not? What future do you see for your idea now?"

Her question caught John like a sucker punch. Not because of any malicious intent, but she was asking the same question John had asked himself all night. What future does his fledgling firm have now?

"The product fills an important need, but I just haven't figured out how to communicate the benefits to others yet. I guess I have a lot of thinking to do this weekend."

Stacy stood on her tiptoes and planted a kiss on his cheek.

"I know this is hard, but you still have to do the right thing. You need to fess up to your mistake with Mr. Fletcher first before he hears about it from someone else. He'll still be mad, but I hope he'd respect your honesty."

The rest of the weekend was a blur to John. He couldn't concentrate on anything else, but he agreed with Stacy. He had

CHAPTER 18

to go to Mr. Fletcher and admit his mistake. John wasn't sure he wanted to give up on Sectronix yet but chose to cross that bridge after he confessed to Karl Fletcher.

Monday morning, John got up before his alarm went off. He got ready for work and arrived early in the empty parking lot. John closed his eyes and prayed. After praying, he kept his eyes closed in his quiet truck to listen for any words from God. His eyes remained closed until he heard a car door shut next to him. The parking lot was a quarter full.

John avoided Raj and Eric all morning. He decided he would stop by Mr. Fletcher's office later in the day to confess. At two o'clock, he received a call from Karl Fletcher's assistant.

"Mr. Fletcher would like to see you in his office now."

"Right now?"

"Yes, please."

John processed dozens of possibilities between his desk and Mr. Fletcher's office in the corner of the building. Did he already hear from Greg Hopkins, or was this for something unrelated?

Mr. Fletcher's assistant told John he could go into his office. John stuck his head inside and saw Mr. Fletcher talking on the phone. He smiled at John and waved him in.

John exhaled and let his shoulders relax. Mr. Fletcher didn't seem angry, so that was a positive sign. John pondered the reason for the unexpected invitation while Mr. Fletcher ended his call. He looked at Mr. Fletcher's desk, and his heart sank.

A business card sat in the middle of his desk.

It was from John Nickerson at Sectronix.

Chapter 19

Mr. Fletcher put down the receiver and smiled at John.

"How was your weekend?" the founder of Fletcher Security asked.

John thought he might get sick and lose his lunch on the cherrywood desk in front of him. The feeling intensified when John realized Mr. Fletcher knew what was going on but was just toying with him. Karl Fletcher was the old country tomcat, and John was the mouse trying to wiggle its tail from his paw.

"Mr. Fletcher, I have something I need to share with you."

Mr. Fletcher leaned back in his chair with a grin. "I bet you do. I'm dying to hear it."

"Well, I wasn't happy that you didn't even consider my suggestions with the German transmitters, so I tried to present them to a potential account myself to validate my idea was good for the company."

Mr. Fletcher's eyebrows raised. "Oh, so you were acting on behalf of Fletcher Security to sell more products for us?"

John wanted to answer in the affirmative. It might be the only way to save his job, but something stopped him. It was the voice he was seeking early that day in the parking lot.

Be honest.

After several seconds of silence, John looked down at the

floor and then exhaled. "No, I was trying to see if it was a good enough idea for me to start a new company."

The smile on Mr. Fletcher's face vanished. "Now, you understand the problem this creates for me. We are paying you to be a software engineer for us, and now you are pitching your products to one of our customers. You are competing against your own employer. My company."

"I'm sorry, Mr. Fletcher. I—"

Mr. Fletcher put his hand up to stop John. "Not as sorry as I am. You are a talented programmer, but a disloyal employee and a lousy entrepreneur. Pack up your items and see that you are out of here in the next fifteen minutes."

John stared at Mr. Fletcher as if he must have heard him wrong.

After a few seconds of uncomfortable silence, Mr. Fletcher leaned over his desk and pointed to his watch. "Tick-tock, John. Get going."

Ten minutes later, John placed two boxes in the backseat of his SUV. He sat in the driver seat and looked at the building he'd likely never enter again.

"What was I thinking? What am I going to do now?"

Chapter 20

John slinked through the back door. Stacy sat at the kitchen table next to Connor with an open textbook. Zach was scribbling on a sheet of paper at the opposite end of the table.

Connor and Zach looked up and greeted him in unison. "Hi, Dad."

"Hey, guys."

Stacy looked at the clock on the oven and then back to John. Her eyes narrowed, and her forehead wrinkled.

"You're home early." It wasn't a question, but more of a confirmation that she knew that something was awry.

John didn't acknowledge the submission of evidence. He darted back to his lab.

Thirty minutes Stacy entered without knocking. John leaned over his plywood table with his fingers through his hair and did not look up. He stared into the woody waves and knots of his work surface. Stacy sat in the same chair that they used to test Sure Cuffs two weeks earlier.

"What's going on?"

John looked up. "They fired me."

He straightened himself for her reaction. Would she be angry? Upset? Both?

"What are you going to do now?" Stacy asked coolly.

CHAPTER 20

John paused before responding. This was not the reaction he was expecting. She didn't even ask why he got fired. Did she understand what he just told her?

"I don't know. I wasn't expecting this to happen."

Stacy stood and moved next to John. Her cheeks turned red, and her mouth was open. "How could you not see this coming? You've been sneaking around with two co-workers trying to launch a competitor to your company. Did Raj and Eric get fired?"

John wasn't sure. He had packed up and left so fast. He hadn't heard from Eric or Raj yet so he assumed they were safe.

"I don't think so. Just me."

Stacy paced next to John. "I'll talk to Dr. Beasley about picking up more hours. That should help get us by until you find a new job."

"I don't want to work for another company."

"What? What do you plan to do?"

"I want to grow Sectronix. I'll turn that into my next full-time job." John whispered.

"Do you have any customers lined up or any money in your business account?"

John shook his head. "No, I don't have any customers yet and I'm almost out of the savings I transferred. I talked to a lender last week about a home equity loan and I think that's our best option."

"You mean a bank loan?" Stacy snapped.

"No, I can't get a bank loan yet. A home equity loan is all I can get."

The redness in Stacy's face extended to her neck and arms. "What about your partners? Are they taking out home equity loans too?"

John exhaled. "No, we agreed that they would invest once we found a customer. They are working for free now, but they haven't invested any money yet."

Stacy stopped pacing.

"Do you realize we could lose the house if we default on a home equity loan?"

John didn't respond. He'd already wrestled with that worst-case scenario since the advisor first suggested it. He was out of options.

John shuffled to the empty chair that Stacy sat in a minute earlier. He fell back into the chair and placed his face into his cupped hands. He knew Stacy was right. It was a major risk, but the feeling that Sure Cuffs was so close to success pulled him like a powerful undertow. He had to fight for one last opportunity.

"I still believe in Sure Cuffs. Can we give it one last shot?" John asked as he looked up at Stacy.

She put her hands on her hips and bent down to reduce the distance between her mouth and his ears. "I feel like you're putting all of this on me. I'm already taking care of the kids full-time while working part-time and now I'm going to be worried about losing our house."

"I'll give it one hundred percent. I don't want to lose the house either."

Stacy turned toward the closed door. "I have to get Zach started on his homework," she barked as she marched out of the room.

John leaned back and bounced his head off the wall. "Why does this have to be so hard?"

A minute later, he had his laptop open, and was busy searching for a solution. He may have to take out a home equity

CHAPTER 20

loan and look for a new job, but he could also try to find a customer for Sectronix. It couldn't be a small test account. His next account had to generate meaningful income to prove to Stacy that Sectronix could be his full-time job.

What account had a genuine need for Sure Cuffs, but also had the budget to provide the revenue Sectronix needed for survival? Government organizations would be the top candidates, and a few of them met the ideal profile. Ten minutes later, John straightened and smiled.

"Of course. They need it as much as any agency, and they have a large office in town."

John had his primary target. It was the US Marshals Service of the Western District of Texas. They transported inmates from other correctional facilities and to court appearances. If the US Marshals had Sure Cuffs, it could prevent another tragedy like Kyle's needless death.

Next, John needed to get an appointment to present Sure Cuffs, and that wouldn't be easy. It didn't matter. John had no choice but to get an appointment.

John waited for Stacy to turn her light out before he went to bed. He crawled in bed in the hope of not waking her.

Stacy sat up. "I've thought more about what you said."

"Me too. I'm sorry I put all this on you."

Stacy ignored his apology. John could tell she had something important to say, so he stopped talking.

"I'll agree to the home equity loan, but with one condition. If your company doesn't have a customer after two months, then you commit one hundred percent to get a new full-time job and stop working on your new business so we can pay back the home equity loan as soon as possible."

John didn't like the prospect of giving up Sectronix after two months, but also realized that was the right thing to do.

"Can you commit to that?"

John paused for a moment and then nodded. "Yeah, I can commit to that. Again, I'm sorry that—"

Stacy slid back down under the covers and turned on her side with her back facing John.

John also slid under the comforter and stared up at the quiet rotation of the ceiling fan. Stacy had supported John's entrepreneurial dream since they first met, but the stakes were higher now. They had a young family to consider, and both John and Stacy were committed to providing a quality life for their three children. It could all come crashing down if Sectronix failed.

Two months was not much time to launch a new business, but John had a slight glimmer of hope.

It was do or die for Sure Cuffs.

Chapter 21

The receptionist asked John if he'd like to leave a message.

"Do you know what time he'll be back at his desk?"

"I don't know, sir. If you leave your name and number, I can ask him to call you back."

"No, thank you. I'll just try again later."

On the third day of calling, both John and the receptionist were getting frustrated with their dance. He didn't want to tell her why he was calling because he assumed they would ignore him like Greg Hopkins at the municipal courthouse. She also sounded frustrated with the same person calling for the director of security multiple times a day, but never leaving his name or number.

"Can I please speak with the director of security," John blurted when the receptionist answered the phone.

"Look, sweetie, most of the people in this office don't answer their phones if they're not expecting a call. Are you sure you don't want to leave your name or your number? I'm not sure you will ever get one of them to pick up the phone to talk to you."

Her honesty was both jarring yet refreshing. The soothing voice of a woman he pictured to be his mother's age disarmed John.

"I'm sorry for being so coy, but I must present something to the director of security. In my experience, nobody ever returns a voicemail."

"Are you trying to become a new vendor? Are you based in Texas?"

"Yes to both."

"Well, you're in luck. We have an open call for Texas-based vendors at the end of every quarter to present new products and services to the purchasing team here at the US Marshals Service. All vendors get fifteen minutes to present their new product or service, and if the team likes it, they'll bring you back for a longer one-to-one meeting. Would you like me to add your name to the list?"

"Absolutely!"

John gave the receptionist the required information. Excitement grew inside him as he considered the prospect of landing the US Marshals office for Sure Cuffs.

"When is the event to pitch the purchasing team?"

"It's in two weeks from tomorrow."

"Two weeks?"

"Does that still work for you?"

"Yes, I was just hoping it was sooner."

"You're lucky a slot was even available. You got the last one. Usually, they're booked up a month or two before the event."

John hung up the phone and pumped his fist. The US Marshals Service was one of his high priority target accounts. They handled the security at many of the judicial buildings and transported most inmates. They were perfect for Sure Cuffs.

For the next two weeks, John spent hours perfecting his pitch. He would have felt better if Raj and Eric could have joined him, but they were still working at Fletcher Security. Both reduced

CHAPTER 21

their public interaction with John after Karl Fletcher fired him. So far, neither were associated with John's act of treason, and they didn't want to create any suspicion of their involvement.

On the day of the presentation, John arrived in the parking lot thirty minutes early. He pulled down the visor and stared into the anxious eyes in the mirror. John blinked several times and then moved closer to the familiar face looking back at him. He inhaled and let out a long, measured breath.

"You've got this."

Once inside the office building, John tugged at his suit jacket to prevent wrinkles while he sat in a stiff chair in the waiting room. Three other groups clustered together in the room while one group presented inside the conference room. The other companies had at least two people, and one was even three members strong.

The steady confidence John exuded in the parking lot waned with each passing minute. Sectronix would present third that hour, so he still had thirty minutes to let his anxiety gnaw at him deeper and deeper.

Thirty minutes felt more like an entire morning, but the conference room doors opened, and a pair of potential vendors whispered to each other as they departed.

A woman in her mid-forties called out into the waiting room: "Sectronix."

John rose and marched into the room. Four judges were sitting on one side of the long board-room style table. Two men and two women. John stood on the opposite side with his back to a video screen to help him present his product.

After he inserted his USB drive into the laptop, the Sure Cuffs logo appeared. John launched into his presentation. He saw the attentive looks and nodding heads to each of his bullet points, and his confidence grew. The presentation ended with five minutes to spare.

"I know this is a unique solution, so I want to leave some time for discussion or questions."

The older of the two men spoke first. "Very impressive, Mr. Nickerson. I can envision some applications where your Sure Cuffs would be a benefit."

"Thank you," John replied.

"How do you outfit an inmate with Sure Cuffs?"

John smiled and took a step closer to the table. "We insert the transmitters under their skin. We've found this provides the safest and most reliable outcomes."

The foursome exchanged glances. This time the woman that called him into the room spoke. "Please understand that we take temporary custody of inmates. I don't see how we could insert something under an inmate's skin when we have custody for a matter of days or even hours. I like the concept, but I don't think it's right for us."

"We can install the transmitters in under twenty minutes." John protested.

"That would still create a logistical and maybe even a legal issue for us. I'm sorry, but Sure Cuffs is not a suitable fit for the US Marshals Service."

John froze. He heard the words but could not process the abrupt rejection after watching the nodding heads moments before.

"Thank you, Mr. Nickerson."

He retrieved his USB drive and shuffled out of the room.

The older gentleman shouted toward John before he left the room. "Try Travis County."

John turned back to face the man.

CHAPTER 21

"Sure Cuffs is better suited for medium to long term incarcerations. Try the Travis County Correctional Complex. I think you'll get a positive response there."

The dejected president of Sectronix tried to return a smile but flashed a forced grin for only a split second. He turned back to the waiting room and trudged out to his SUV. John shut the door and let the silence wash over him.

"I thought for sure the Marshals Service would want Sure Cuffs. It could have prevented another death like Kyle's," he muttered.

John started the engine and thought more about the older man's suggestion.

Perhaps a traditional jail system was a better fit for Sure Cuffs. John would search for a contact at the Travis County Correctional Complex when he got home.

Now he only had six weeks left until his deadline with Stacy.

Chapter 22

John found the name of the person responsible for security at Travis County Corrections on their website. He called Kathy Watson just after nine the next morning.

The front desk attendant patched John through, and he took a sip of coffee while he waited for the voicemail.

"This is Kathy."

John was so surprised that a human answered the phone and he spit out his coffee. He recovered and launched into his sixty-second pitch.

Mrs. Watson was silent for a few seconds before she spoke. "Who else is using this product?"

"Ms. Watson, Travis County would be the first."

"Please call me Kathy."

"Okay, Kathy, I presented it to the US Marshals Service earlier this week, and they liked it, but they recommended I contact you. They said it would be an excellent fit for Travis County Corrections Complex."

It felt good to name drop. John knew now that going to the US Marshals Service first was worth the effort even though they declined to purchase Sure Cuffs.

"Isn't that nice of them to pass along a salesman to me? I'll have to send them a Christmas card this year."

CHAPTER 22

"They just thought you were a good fit."

"Oh, I know. It sounds interesting. How long do you need?"

John's heart sped up. He shuffled around a couple of pieces of paper. An hour would be ideal, but was that asking for too much?

"Thirty minutes would be great."

"I am open next Thursday from eight to eight-thirty or the following week at—"

"I'll take eight o'clock next Thursday, thank you."

"Okay, be here at least fifteen minutes early so the front desk can check you in."

John ended the call and tossed his phone on his desk. He trotted into the kitchen and found Abby eating breakfast alone.

"Morning, sunshine. Where's Mom?"

"She took the boys to the bus stop."

John ruffled her hair and watched the sidewalk for Stacy to appear. He waited for her to enter the house and handed her a fresh mug of coffee.

"What's this for?" Stacy asked with a suspicious smile.

"I landed a presentation with the large prison complex out by the airport next Thursday. This could be the account that launches Sure Cuffs."

Stacy's smile turned genuine. "That's great."

It was the act of support John desperately needed.

"I'll need you to drop off Abby at daycare around nine every day and pick the boys up from soccer practice after school. The coach wants all parents to be there for pickup by four-thirty."

"Every day? I have an important presentation to prepare."

Stacy's smile evaporated. "I told you I would pick up additional hours because you're not working. They scheduled me four days this week and next, and you're not going into the office anymore. So yes, I need your help every day."

John heard Stacy's reply, and he also felt it. He knew he was putting a lot more pressure on his wife, and her responsibilities didn't stop because of his job loss or a future appointment. He needed to step up.

"Okay. I'll take all drop-offs and pickups for the next two weeks, but can you drop off Abby next Thursday? My meeting is at seven-thirty."

"I can't. Can you ask them to move the meeting back?"

John didn't want to risk any changes to his current appointment. It was too important. But another solution struck him. "You know, I can ask Kayla if she can take Abby. She's always offering to help so I'm sure she would do it."

"That's fine. I'll leave it up to you to work it out with Kayla. I'm going to be late, so please help Abby get her shoes on and take her today."

Stacy left the kitchen, and John turned to Abby. "It's just you and me, kid."

Abby raised her arms in victory. "Yeah."

John wished he had her confidence in his ability.

"We are going to stop by Auntie Kayla and Uncle Frank's house, so we need to leave in a few minutes."

John called Kayla on the way and she was waiting outside when he pulled up. Abby jumped out and ran up to her aunt. She opened her arms and gave Auntie Kayla a big hug.

"Who's my favorite niece?"

"Me!" Abby said, pointing to herself.

John joined Kayla on the sidewalk. "Is Frank already at work?"

"Yeah, you just missed him."

"Tell him I said hi."

CHAPTER 22

"I will," Kayla promised.

"I'm taking Abby to daycare today, but would you be able to take her on Thursday?"

"I'd love to. Why? What's going on?"

"You know how I've told you about my new company Sectronix and my Sure Cuffs product?"

"Yeah, I remember."

John leaned up against his SUV. "Well, I have a big meeting with the Travis County Corrections Complex out by the airport early Thursday."

"That's exciting news. I'll pray for you."

They both turned to watch Abby gliding back and forth on the swing on the front porch.

"Thanks. I'm showing them the product that was inspired by Kyle. I think about him every day and still hope I can prevent someone else from enduring the same pain as us." John's voice cracked as he replied.

Tears welled up in Kayla's eyes until one escaped and dashed across her cheek. She walked toward John with her arms open. "Thank you," she said while they embraced. "I'll take Abby on Thursday and you sell a million units of your product to that prison."

Similar to the US Marshals Service meeting, John would have to present solo. He prepared his presentation and pitch for hours every day between chauffeur duties. On Wednesday before the meeting, John met with Raj and Eric at a sports bar on Sixth Street after they got off work. John did a dry run of his presentation with the small Sectronix team. They both added suggestions, but overall thought it was ready for John to deliver to Travis County.

As instructed, John arrived early at the Travis County Correctional Complex. He didn't tell Kathy, but he was familiar with TCCC because of the meeting earlier in the year when his former co-worker Amber was nearly assaulted during a tour. This time John would enter as Sectronix and not Fletcher Security, a liberating feeling.

Kathy arrived at precisely eight o'clock to escort John back to her office. John figured Kathy to be in her early forties. She dressed in professional attire with black pants and a blazer over her cream-colored shirt. He noticed she walked with a slight limp as she led him to her cramped office.

Kathy moved a stack of files to the other side of her desk so John could sit on the corner and present on his laptop.

Like his presentation to the US Marshals Service, John ended early to allow time for discussion or questions.

Kathy reviewed her notes for several seconds before speaking. "Mr. Nickerson, what is your aim with Sure Cuffs?"

John straightened in his chair. "I'd like every detention center in America to use Sure Cuffs for all inmates with medium to long-term sentences."

Kathy nodded. "What about this complex? What is your goal?"

"I'd like for you to be the first institution to use Sure Cuffs and become the model for all other facilities."

Kathy circled something on her notepad and tapped on it with her pen. "Are you willing to provide free materials and support for a test?"

The question was not unexpected, but it still made John shift in his chair. It made sense for Travis County, but testing would exhaust two resources he had very little of: time and money. After a quick internal debate, John understood he only had one choice.

CHAPTER 22

"Yes, I can support a two-week test."

"We'd need at least a month. Maybe more."

John shifted in his chair again. "I'll do whatever it takes for Travis County to feel comfortable enough to sign a contract for Sure Cuffs."

"Great. I'll share this with my supervisor and get back to you with any questions."

John called Raj and then Eric on his way home. He shared the positive response from Kathy and told them he'd need their help if Travis County wanted to test Sure Cuffs.

Now it was a waiting game. John looked at his phone so many times every hour, time seemed to stop. The wait was grueling, but John had no way to speed up their decision. His deadline to back burner Sectronix and start job hunting was five weeks away. Each passing day added more weight on John's shoulders. He wasn't sure how much more he could bear.

Chapter 23

John's phone rang on his desk. He turned it over and saw it was from an unrecognized 512 area code. He answered it after the second ring.

"Hi, John, this is Kathy from the Travis County Correctional Complex. How are you?"

John swallowed hard. "I'm well. How about you?"

"I'm calling with good news. We'd like to test Sure Cuffs on eight inmates for the next month. We can get started the week after next."

That would push the test beyond John's deadline to generate revenue for Sectronix, but it didn't matter. This was his only option, and if the test was going well, John suspected that Stacy would be okay with a short extension.

"Outstanding! What should I do next?"

Kathy explained the new vendor set-up process and scheduled another call the following week to ensure everything would be ready to test on time.

"Thanks again for this opportunity. I look forward to demonstrating the unique benefits of Sure Cuffs during the test," John shared before the call ended.

He jumped from his chair and began pacing in his lab.

"Okay, the actual work can begin now."

CHAPTER 23

John texted Raj and Eric with the news. They agreed to meet that night after John dropped the boys off at home after practice.

The trio exchanged high fives at their high-top table at the Hill Country Grille. Full-time employment, beating Fletcher Security in future RFPs and divvying up stock after a Sectronix IPO were discussed as if success was assured. John brought the discussion back to reality.

"We have a lot of work to do to pull off this test. Kathy gave me particular instructions."

John gave Eric and Raj a play-by-play review of Kathy's instructions.

"I know you two can't be there because of work, but we need to divide up the responsibilities. I'll work on all the paperwork they requested. Eric, I need you to gather and test all the hardware. We need to be one hundred percent sure it will work. Raj, you need to work on the apps for the corrections officers and test the software. Triple test it. We can't afford any mistakes during this test."

The Sectronix team tested every piece of hardware and line of code for Sure Cuffs multiple times before John's launch date at TCCC. John turned in the required paperwork and insurance documentation three days early. The moment of truth arrived for John and Sectronix.

John met again in the plush boardroom with a small team from Travis County. They shared their standard protocol for testing new products and services with him.

"We agreed to test Sure Cuffs on eight inmates who volunteered to participate in return for external work privileges. They will be part of a group that does chain gang type work in the community, so Sure Cuffs is ideal for that group of inmates."

Three hours later, John left the complex. He finished

inserting the Sure Cuffs transmitters into all eight inmates and uploaded the app on the phones of the designated corrections officers. After John trained the TCCC staff on how to use the Sure Cuffs app, the test period began.

The first week was a complete success for Sectronix. Correction officers only had to activate Sure Cuffs once after an inmate refused to get back on the bus at the end of the workday. The second week also started out on a positive note after an officer activated Sure Cuffs to break up a scuffle between two inmates. In his incident report, the officer reported that he felt Sure Cuffs protected him from potential harm from the inmates because he didn't have to get physically involved in the skirmish. One tap of the app and both inmates fell to the ground immobilized.

Excitement grew in John with each passing day. His dream of starting a new business with one of his ideas was becoming a reality. Success inched closer and appeared to be on the horizon. John couldn't wait for the four-week test to end and to cross the finish line and declare Sure Cuffs a winner.

Two weeks into the test, John looked in his rear-view mirror at his three children in the back seat. He just picked up Zack and Connor from soccer practice and was on his way home. *Sectronix will help me give them the life they deserve.*

John smiled at the thought of passing along his business to his children when his phone rang.

"John, this is Kathy. We had a major problem with Sure Cuffs."

"What is it?"

"We have to terminate the test of Sure Cuffs early. We had a serious malfunction today, and the team doesn't feel comfortable proceeding with the test. Can you come in first thing tomorrow?"

CHAPTER 23

John agreed and hung up at the same time he pulled into his driveway. All three kids unbuckled their seat belts and ran inside, leaving John alone in his SUV.

"What just happened?"

Two minutes earlier, John was thinking about starting a legacy with a family business, and now the same company appeared to be doomed. He couldn't imagine what could have gone wrong.

He didn't tell anyone else about the call from TCCC. John stared up at the ceiling through the darkness the entire night. He didn't sleep a single minute. He had to find out what went wrong.

The conference room at the Travis County Correctional Complex felt smaller and warmer to John than previous meetings. The mood was somber. John sensed it also disappointed the TCCC team that Sure Cuffs did not work. That made the sting of the meeting penetrate even deeper into his bones.

The meeting began with Kathy explaining the reason for the emergency meeting. Next, the corrections officer on the scene of the incident shared his account of the malfunction.

"We were doing trash collection along the freeway next to a church building. The church had a couple dozen kids out playing in their playground, so I notified the inmates of a boundary at the speed limit sign. I told them that nobody was to go past the sign."

The youthful man in his late twenties took a sip of his coffee and continued. "Well, everything was fine for the first hour, and we were fixin' to leave soon when I saw three inmates close to the boundary. I gave a verbal warning not to pass the sign, but all three kept walking without breaking their stride. I jogged a few steps toward them, and when I saw they were all five or six steps past the sign heading toward the kids, I hit activate on the Sure Cuffs app. Seven of the inmates froze, and two of the inmates past the sign fell, but one inmate didn't stop moving. He started acting funny."

John's forehead wrinkled, and Kathy noticed. "Officer, what do you mean by acting funny?"

"I mean, he was flopping around like a rabid bobcat. His arms and legs were flying around in different directions. One second his right arm would cross over to his left side, and then it would shoot down to his legs. A few seconds later, the inmate fell to the ground, but he kept flopping around, so I deactivated the Sure Cuffs, and it stopped. It scared the dickens out of all of us."

Kathy turned to a member of the TCCC medical staff. "What did you find when the inmate returned?"

The bespectacled, white-haired woman responded with a quick and sharp report. "We found that the inmate had been digging at the transmitters with his fingernails. He dug deep enough to damage them, and they malfunctioned when the app was activated."

John's thoughts drifted as the meeting continued. He couldn't believe his dream could evaporate because of a guy digging into his arms and legs with his fingernails. John felt more nauseated each minute the meeting continued. He took deep, quiet breaths to combat his urge to throw up.

Ten minutes later, Kathy spoke. "John, we are sorry this didn't work out, but as you can see, we cannot continue to test Sure Cuffs at this facility anymore."

That was it. The meeting was over, and so was John's dream.

Chapter 24

The drive home from TCCC felt like an eternity. The last twenty-four hours were a nasty dream for John, a nightmare in which he couldn't wake up.

He arrived home to an empty house. Stacy wouldn't be back for another five hours, and John needed the time to process his latest setback. The second payment on his home equity loan was due in two weeks and his balance in his bank account was going the wrong direction. Plus, he had no leads.

John leaned back in his desk chair until he was facing the ceiling. He watched the movie of the meeting at TCCC in his mind again and still couldn't fathom his lousy luck.

What am I doing wrong? Did I pick the wrong product to launch? Was Sure Cuffs really ready to launch? Or was the problem me?

His last question hung in his mind like a thick fog. Everything else seemed to be ready but him. He launched his new business sooner than expected after getting fired from his job. John was the weak link to his own company. He'd fire himself now if he could.

John opened his laptop and browser. He found a website with local job listings and scrolled through them for his next potential job.

"Yuck! I can't go back to this."

John paced in his lab. He talked aloud as he pondered his final options.

"I've got to find an account willing to move fast. It will have to be a smaller account, but it can be a springboard to a larger account."

John spent the rest of the afternoon searching for potential accounts in the State of Texas and Oklahoma. He considered widening his net even farther because he had to find the right account—any account that could agree to Sure Cuffs in less than two weeks.

The list of potential accounts grew to three pages on his legal pad when he heard the back door open. John walked out and met Stacy and Abby.

"Hey."

Stacy looked at the clock. "Are you picking up the boys?"

"Yes, I'm leaving right now," John replied as he lurched toward his keys on the counter. He darted out of the door before Stacy could say anything else. John would be ten minutes late, and the coach would have to stay with them. His boys would lose playing time because of his mistake.

John arrived home thirty minutes later. Stacy slammed the refrigerator and cabinet doors as she prepared a snack for Connor and Zack. John thought it would be best to vanish, but she caught him trying to sneak out.

"Why were you so late getting the boys? You weren't even planning to leave until you saw me. You've been home all afternoon, and you didn't even have to drop off today. Is it too much to ask you to do one thing for me?"

Stacy's words grew louder with each question. At first, John wanted to defend himself. Tell her how busy he was as he worked to keep his new company afloat. However, he didn't

CHAPTER 24

have the energy to defend his actions.

"I lost Travis County. I don't have anything else pending."

Stacy's face returned to its traditional color, and she stared back at John with her mouth open.

"I was trying to find a new option. I'm sorry, I lost track of time."

"Let's go talk." Stacy led John into the family room. She sat down and motioned for him to do the same.

"What happened?"

John explained the entire story. He spoke slowly as if he was trying to remember the details of a dream.

Stacy turned toward him after he finished. "I know how hard you worked to launch this company, but do you think it's time to throw in the towel now?"

John's head snapped from the dark TV to Stacy. "Throw in the towel?"

"Should you look for your next job now?

"I still have two weeks until my deadline."

Stacy went into the kitchen and returned with an open envelope that she handed to John. He pulled the one-page invoice and scanned the contents until he reached the bottom of the page.

"Two thousand dollars for health insurance? That's crazy."

"That's how much it costs for insurance through COBRA. We need health insurance so we can expect that extra expense every month now," Stacy whispered.

John continued to stare at the sheet of paper that shoveled more dirt on the grave of his entrepreneurial dreams.

"I don't know how we can afford COBRA plus a payment on the home equity loan without using the home equity funds to pay it. I want to pay that loan off as soon as possible, not keep digging ourselves deeper into debt."

John dropped his face into his cupped hands. He exhaled and ran his fingers through his hair. "So we may go without healthcare, potentially lose our house or be forced to shut down Sectronix unless I find a new job. Those are our options?"

Stacy frowned. "I'm afraid so."

John turned back to the wall with the TV.

He didn't respond, so Stacy stood up. "I'll leave you alone so you can think about what you want to do."

There it was. The crossroads John was dreading. He didn't want to veer off his current course, but that route had all but disappeared for John.

His chance to save his dream of starting his own business was down to its last hour.

Chapter 25

The next morning, John cut the grass, trimmed the shrubs, and swept the sidewalk after he dropped off Abby at daycare. He tried to do anything that would help him avoid scouring online job sites. John wasn't desperate enough to paint the shed, so he went inside his lab and closed the door.

He sat down in his office chair and curled his hands into fists. Next, John closed his eyes and bent over until his head was resting on his fists near his knees. He prayed harder and longer than he could ever remember. John prayed for forgiveness for putting so much stress on Stacy. He prayed for guidance so he would honor God's will and not his own with his next job. He prayed for a miracle and for one last chance to achieve his dream for Sure Cuffs.

John sat still while he waited to see if Jesus had any guidance for him.

Ping.

John's phone broke the silence in the room. He opened his eyes and had to blink several times to adjust to the light. It was a text from an unknown number.

Hi John, I hope you remember me. It's Amber. We used to work together at Fletcher Security. I talked to Eric yesterday and he said I should speak to you. Call me.

He remembered Amber, the former finance manager, who was nearly attacked by an inmate when they went on a site visit to TCCC earlier in the year.

"I wonder what she wants."

John recalled she had been in the finance department with Eric, so maybe they were friends. He knew she left the company not long after the incident at TCCC but had not spoken with Amber since she left Fletcher Security. He dialed her number, and she answered in one ring.

The two former Fletcher Security employees exchanged greetings, and then John cut to the chase.

"So, Eric recommended that you should text me?"

"Yes, I've kept in touch with Eric since I left, and he told me you got fired last month. I couldn't believe it because you were one of the few good guys there."

John smiled.

"I asked why you got let go, and he told me about the new product you created and how you are trying to find new accounts when Mr. Fletcher found out."

"He told you all that?"

"Yeah, don't worry. Let's just say I'm not sending any Christmas cards to the Fletcher family. I may be able to help you though. Would you be interested?"

This conversation was coming at John so fast he wasn't sure what to make of it. After a few seconds, he summoned enough oxygen to respond. "Sure, I'd love to hear how you can help."

"Well, I went back to sales after I left Fletcher. I'm at a broadline distributor of food, cleaning supplies, and stuff like that. One of my largest accounts is the Hays County Jail, and the VP of purchasing is an old friend of mine."

Still unsure of the purpose of the call, John could only muster

CHAPTER 25

"okay" for a response.

"Would you like me to introduce you to her? I have a standing meeting with her team every Tuesday, so I'd be happy to introduce you at my next meeting if you're willing to drive down to San Marcos."

John jumped off his chair to respond. "Wow, Amber, that would be great. That'd be a tremendous help."

John looked down at the invoice for health insurance on his desk and remembered what Eric said at the Hill Country Grille weeks ago. He had to be aggressive. The existence of Sectronix and Sure Cuffs depended on it.

Desperation kicked in and John swung for the fences.

"Amber, you have already done so much for me that I could never repay you, but I have another huge favor to ask."

"Sure, shoot."

"Instead of an introduction, could you see if your contact would gather her team for a twenty-minute presentation on Sure Cuffs next week? I'm in a major time crunch right now."

Amber was quiet for several seconds. "I don't know, John. It's only a few days away, and I don't want to just spring it on her. Maybe we—"

Amber stopped mid-sentence and was quiet again. Five seconds later, she responded with excitement. "You know what, let's do it. I have an hour, so I'll give you the first twenty minutes. Eric said this Sure Cuffs product was a game-changer for the industry, so I'm looking forward to hearing more about it."

They made plans to meet before the presentation, and John hung up the phone. He couldn't believe how his luck swung in his favor over the last hour.

John texted Eric and Raj to tell them the news. He thanked Eric for telling Amber and told both of them he'd give them an update after the meeting. Their response was the second unexpected shock of the morning.

They both wanted to come with John to the presentation. Eric and Raj would take personal days from work so they could join him and support Sectronix. John texted Raj and asked why.

We know this is our last chance. We want to be with you to fight for Sure Cuffs.

John felt a deep sense of gratitude for the loyalty of Eric and Raj.

The eager trio worked on their presentation for hours over the weekend. They role-played questions the staff at Hays County might ask in the meeting and mutually agreed on the best responses to key questions. They believed they were ready to wow the purchasing team at the Hays County Jail. After lunch on Tuesday, they all met at John's house. They drove together down to San Marcos to meet Amber and present Sure Cuffs.

The Sectronix team followed Amber into a conference room. The Hays County team had four people situated around the large table. John moved to the front of the room while Eric and Raj filled in the empty chairs near the back of the boardroom table.

John confirmed that the projector worked and turned to Amber. She nodded, and John began his presentation. For the next twenty minutes, the Sectronix team worked like a seasoned pit crew. Raj and Eric chimed in to elaborate on the response if John didn't answer the question with the witty answer they rehearsed.

After their performance, John sat down and exchanged a quick smile with his team. He turned to the Hays County Jail members.

CHAPTER 25

"Can I answer any questions for you?"

The older woman in the group turned to the others on her team. Her curly gray hair bounced with each new direction she turned.

"I'm confused about what you are trying to sell us. Are you selling the transmitters or the app?"

John smiled. "We are selling both. Sure Cuffs is a complete security package that enables your corrections staff to have absolute command over your inmates."

Wrinkles appeared on her forehead. "How much does it cost?"

John shifted his weight in his chair and tried his best to maintain a smile. He could see Eric tug at his shirt collar as his neck and cheeks turned red. Raj was expressionless.

"Sure Cuffs is a subscription service. We charge a monthly fee per inmate, which includes all the transmitters, app, monitoring, and support."

The woman raised her hands above her head like she was signaling a field goal in a local high school football game. She wasn't playing a game though. Her exasperation at the whole idea of Sure Cuffs was evident to everyone in the room.

"I'm not sure what the point is here. We already have restraints that last for years, so why would we pay more money for something that does the same thing?"

She looked around to gather support for her crusade, but the other three people from Hays County were busy studying their notes. John sensed they had seen this storm before and were just waiting for it to pass.

John could no longer maintain a smile. He looked at Amber at the far end of the table, and she mouthed, "I'm sorry."

Eric was next to Amber. His eyes were bulging, and he rocked back and forth. John thought Eric might jump out of his chair any minute. It occurred to John that he'd seen a temper in Eric before when he would accompany Karl Fletcher on a mission to terrorize an employee on his hit list.

John cleared his throat. "I'm sorry you see it that way, but Sure Cuffs is so much more than traditional restraints. It's the latest—"

A loud voice and movement interrupted him.

"I can't listen to this anymore!" Eric yelled as he stood up and stormed toward the conference room door. Steps before he reached the door, he stopped and turned to face the room full of people with mouths wide open. "I don't know how much more clear and obvious it could be. This is crazy."

Eric turned again to the exit, and after two steps, his body stiffened. His arms and legs slammed to his side, and he fell against the wall and slid down.

At first, nobody moved, and then everyone stood up to see Eric lying on his side on the floor posed like a soldier standing at attention.

"That, ladies and gentlemen, is how Sure Cuffs works," Raj said from the back of the room with his finger still on the activate button on his phone.

"As you can see, Sure Cuffs immobilized a man of Eric's stature within a split second of hitting this button. Now I'll deactivate Sure Cuffs so you can see that he is okay and has no lasting effects of the activation."

Eric pulled his arms away from his body and shook them out. Everyone looked at Eric getting up from the floor in awe after the exhibition they witnessed.

John looked back at Raj. He winked at John.

After the meeting was over, they all walked back to John's SUV in the parking lot. They were recounting the roller coaster

CHAPTER 25

of a meeting as they climbed inside.

Amber intercepted them before they shut the doors. "Impressive performance back there. I can't believe they agreed to thirty licenses of Sure Cuffs on the spot. That skit to activate Sure Cuffs was pure genius. I may need to get some sales tips from you guys."

John thanked Amber again for the invitation, and the Sectronix team departed the Hays County Jail complex. Once on I-35, John turned on his cruise control and glanced over to Eric in the front seat.

"That was great back there, but I have to ask, whose idea was it to send Eric into a rage so you could activate Sure Cuffs?"

Eric continued to look straight ahead at the road. John looked in the rear-view mirror and locked eyes with Raj. He broke his gaze and looked down.

"What's going on, guys?"

Chapter 26

Raj looked up and patted Eric on the back. "Why don't you tell him, Eric?"

Eric turned toward John. "It wasn't an act. I was angry at that lady. It was like fingers on a chalkboard with every dumb question she asked. I'm sorry, I won't let that happen again."

"So how did Raj know to activate Sure Cuffs before you left the room?"

Eric pointed to the backseat with his thumb. "Ask him."

Raj leaned forward over the seat between John and Eric. "I guess it was just an impulse. I had the Sure Cuffs app open on my phone in case anyone wanted to see it. When Eric stood up and started toward the door, I looked down at my phone and saw the big green activate button. Then I remembered the tests on Eric at your house. I wasn't sure it would work, but when he stopped to yell at her one more time, I pushed the button. As they say, the rest is history."

The next week during their meeting at Hill Country Grille, the three members of the Sectronix team discussed the future of the company.

"I want to thank you again for all your help with Sectronix. We are a company with revenue now and I couldn't have done it without you," John stated with a wide smile.

CHAPTER 26

"It was a pleasure to be part of the team that made it happen," Eric said.

John raised his glass and Raj and Eric did the same.

"Now that we have revenue and some hope for the future, it's time for you two to invest in Sectronix and become official partners."

John pushed a folded piece of paper with a number on it to both Eric and Raj.

"That's the investment I'll need from both of you to join Sectronix as a minority owner."

Eric and Raj each unfolded the paper and looked at the number and then at each other. Eric nodded and Raj smiled.

"This is fair. I'm in." Raj said.

"Me too," Eric replied.

"I wish I would have come to you sooner for this investment, but I let pride get in the way, and it created a lot more stress for my wife than I ever wanted. The three of us are a team and I was trying to do it all myself. That won't happen again."

After the meeting, John drove home knowing he was the majority owner of a company based on one of his ideas. A sense of peace filled John for the first time in months.

When John pulled into his driveway, he noticed Frank's truck was parked at the end. Frank and Kayla got out when John's headlights illuminated their rear window.

John furrowed his brow as he put his SUV in park. "Hmm. I wonder why Frank and Kayla are here."

As soon as John exited his vehicle, Frank and Kayla were there to greet him.

"Is everything okay?" John asked.

"Yeah, everything is fine," Frank replied as he shook John's hand.

Kayla looked up to Frank, and he nodded.

"I want to make this quick before I break down crying, but we want you to have this." Kayla handed John a check.

He looked at the amount on the check. "What's this for?"

Kayla smiled. "Frank and I want to invest in your company. This was money we saved for Kyle to go to college, but we can't invest in him now, so we want to invest in you. We really appreciate what you are doing."

John handed the check back to Kayla. "I'm sorry, but this is too much. I can't take this."

"Kyle would want you to have this. Would you say no to him?" Frank asked.

Lips quivered, eyes reddened, and tears flowed. John put the check in his pocket and the three embraced for a full minute.

Two months after securing the Hays County account, the Sectronix team added more county jails in Louisiana, Oklahoma, and North Carolina. Even with the additional income, it still was not enough to support all of them full time, so John set his sights on a new prize. The corrections crown jewel of Texas: The Texas Department of Criminal Justice.

A month later, John met with the deputy director of purchasing at the Texas Department of Criminal Justice multiple times, and they agreed he should present in front of the full board of deputy directors. He prepared for weeks and arrived early for his presentation.

While he was setting up, John noticed a young man who looked to be a few years his junior arrive several minutes early for the presentation. The early guest sat in the farthest corner of the room as if he wanted to remain anonymous. John watched the man as he scratched on his notepad and waited for others to arrive. He'd met other directors in his previous meetings

CHAPTER 26

in the building and this man was different from everyone else he'd met.

John sensed that he also served time in the military based on his hair cut and how he carried himself, but that was not it. He felt this mystery man hiding in the back of the room was going to make a big impact in his life but wasn't sure how. Not yet.

~ The End

Dangerous Redemption Collection

Read how the suspense ratchets up several notches as Sure Cuffs moves from a controlled test environment to the guest bedroom in the home of a young family and their new maximum-security inmate in ***Inviting Danger***.

Inviting Danger: A Christian Suspense Novel

A maximum-security inmate. A young family. Under one roof.

Corrections officer Rey Mendoza's decades-old dream of systemic prison reform appears to be within reach when he accepts a new position. He'll not only better provide for his son's special needs, but also carry forward his father's failed mission.

It's a grave miscalculation.

His ideal job requires hosting an unwelcome house guest — an inmate from a maximum-security prison. As a former prison guard, Rey can handle the imminent threat, but can his wife and two young children endure living under the same roof?

Rey hangs on tight to his mission for prison reform only to see it slip further away. His once-promising dream becomes a nightmare. If he can't find a solution, fast, Rey must abandon everything he's worked for to protect his family from the danger he invited into his home.

Inviting Danger is the first book in the Dangerous Redemption Collection from author Robert Goluba.

Connect With Me

Join My New Release Text List

Text **NEW** to **(844) 465-7100** to receive a text notification of each of my new releases. Nothing else. Ever.

Sign up for the new release and promotion notification newsletter at: **RobertGoluba.com/newletter**

About the Author

Robert Goluba is an author of Christian Suspense. He was born and raised in Central Illinois, where he attended college, served in the Army National Guard, and met his wife. At age thirty, after a self-diagnosed allergy to snow, he moved to sunny Arizona where he now lives with his wonderful wife, two kids, and canine companion.

Also by Robert Goluba

Robert Goluba has published two books in the Dangerous Redemption Christian Suspense Collection, Inviting Danger (Book 1) and Last Second Chance (Book 2), as well as a collection of short stories based on Bible parables called Hope Refreshed

Made in the USA
Coppell, TX
08 November 2021